P9-CBI-419

GRIZZLY PEAK

Jonathan London

Illustrated by

Sean London

WESTWINDS
PRESS®

Text © 2017 by Jonathan London
Illustrations © 2017 by Sean London

All rights reserved. No part of this book may be reproduced or transmitted in any form or by any means, electronic or mechanical, including photocopying, recording, or by any information storage and retrieval system, without written permission of the publisher.

Library of Congress Cataloging-in-Publication Data

Names: London, Jonathan, 1947- author. | London, Sean, illustrator.
Title: Grizzly Peak / Jonathan London ; illustrated by Sean London.
Description: Portland, Oregon : WestWinds Press, 2017. | Series: Aaron's
  Wilderness | Summary: "Aaron's latest adventure takes him river kayaking
  with his dad and tests his perseverance, patience and survival skills in
  encounters with bears, moose, and life-threatening accidents."— Provided
  by publisher. | Sequel to: Bella Bella.
Identifiers: LCCN 2016032969 (print) | LCCN 2016046781 (ebook) | ISBN
  9781943328772 (pbk.) | ISBN 9781943328840 (e-book) | ISBN
  9781943328857 (hardbound)
Subjects: | CYAC: Adventure and adventurers—Fiction. | Outdoor
  life—Fiction. | Fathers and sons—Fiction. | Nature—Fiction.
Classification: LCC PZ7.L8432 Gri 2017 (print) | LCC PZ7.L8432 (ebook) |
DDC
  [Fic]—dc23
LC record available at https://lccn.loc.gov/2016032969

Editor: Michelle McCann
Designer: Vicki Knapton

Published by WestWinds Press®
An imprint of

GRAPHIC ARTS
BOOKS®

P.O. Box 56118
Portland, Oregon 97238-6118
www.graphicartsbooks.com

For Aaron and Sean and Steph, Roger and Lisa, and sweet Maureen. With thanks to my editor Michelle McCann, my publisher Doug Pfeiffer, and to the tireless staff at Graphic Arts: Kathy, Vicki, and Angela.

—Jonathan London

For Jonathan, Maureen, Aaron, and sweet Stephanie. Special thanks to Michelle McCann, Douglas Pfeiffer, and the whole team at Graphic Arts. You have all helped me grow!

—Sean London

CONTENTS

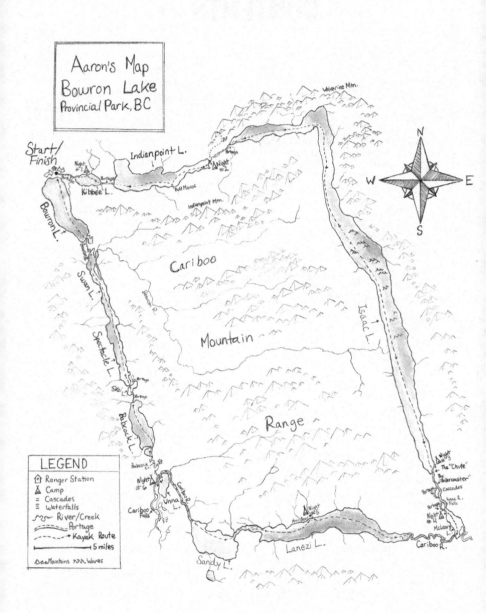

PROLOGUE

Three weeks before I was to graduate from eighth grade, I got kicked out of school.

Expelled.

Long story short, when the principal, Mr. Hyde, rifled through my daypack and found a Swiss Army knife, he didn't want to hear any explanations.

Zero tolerance.

Dad had given me the knife for my birthday. We had gone on two wilderness trips with friends in the last two years—to Desolation Canyon in the Rockies and Bella Bella off the Northwest Coast—and he thought it was time I had a knife, with a can opener, a bottle opener, scissors, tweezers, a tiny saw blade—everything but the kitchen sink.

He had given me the Swiss Army knife when he was proud of me. But that pride had eroded over the past few months. I think it boiled down to change.

I was changing and he was not.

For one thing, I was getting into hip-hop, and trying my hand at writing rap songs, and one of my heroes of the moment was Macklemore. Dad liked my writing—I'd gotten good grades in school for some poems and papers I'd written.

But *rap?* No way! "Too many swearwords," he'd say. It all sounded the same to him. This made me angry. He always wanted me to listen to *his* music, but he never wanted to listen to mine.

And now my grades were going down. The teachers droned on and on, and I got bored. Dad said: "No TV until you start bringing your grades back up." Thanks, Dad.

And I was staying out too late. Hanging with my friends at *their* houses—where their parents were chill. Listening to hip-hop. Even laying down some beats. Or skating on our boards 'til way past dark. Dad said: "You should be doing your homework, Aaron. Not wasting your life!"

What makes him *King?* King of what's good and what's right?

When I quit the flag football team and soccer, that made Dad angry, which made me angry. I liked sports, and wasn't bad at them. But I'd moved on. Those things just didn't interest me anymore. My little brother, Sean, was great at sports. And good at school.

Good for him.

But I was gravitating toward new things, new friends.

I think maybe I was kind of rebelling. When my dad was my age, he was a hippy. I guess that was his way of rebelling, way back then. But now he's like most dads. He wants his kids to excel—NOT rebel.

He didn't like the kids I was hanging with. They didn't do sports. They wanted to make music. I couldn't do anything right. Dad's like, "How's school, Aaron?" and I'd just mumble something and shrug. Or he'd ask why I don't like sports anymore, and I'd shrug. It was too hard to explain. He just didn't get it.

So when I got kicked out of school it was the last straw.

Oh, he knew that I wasn't going to do anything with my knife, and that I'd just forgotten about it still being in my daypack since our fishing trip over spring break. What he couldn't understand was: how could I *forget*?

Like I said, it was the last straw.

Okay, maybe it was the last straw for the principal, too. I kept getting sent to the office for little things.

Wearing my baseball hat in class.

Eating snacks in the library.

Putting my feet up on the desk.

Arriving late.

Not paying attention.

Not doing homework.

I wasn't hurting anybody. I didn't understand what the big deal was.

But Dad—he said it was an *attitude* problem. "Right," I

said. "*Your* attitude, dude!" He didn't like me calling him "dude." I'd started to call him that after hanging out with my friend Cassidy on those wild trips we'd taken. Cassidy said "dude" just about every other word. It drove Dad nuts.

He said: "You're acting like a teenager!"

I said: "Dude, I *am* a teenager!"

I think what was really ticking me off the most was that now Dad was always around. Here. The house. The textbook company he worked for started letting him work from home.

Suddenly he was always here when I got home from school. But either Dad was too busy to even notice me, or—worse—he was in my face.

Turn down that awful thumping sound!

Clean up your room.

Clean up your act!

Maybe you should join the chess club.

You get the picture.

The day after I got expelled, Mom got me a counselor. Sam Somebody. Ponytail and goatee. Old hippy, like Dad. Nice guy. But after I ignored him for a while, he got this crazy idea that he thought would be "good for me."

He told Mom about a camp out in Montana—Camp Wonderland—where they teach "non-recalcitrant (look it up!) juveniles" wilderness survival skills. "Turns them around," the counselor says. "Builds their self-confidence."

Mom didn't know, but I'd heard about camps like these

from Cassidy. He said they are guarded and fenced in with barbed wire, and are out in the middle of nowhere.

I freaked out when Mom told me about it. "I think it might be for the best, sweetie." I knew she loved me but this was really, truly, twisted!

"I'm not going! You can't make me go!"

That's when Dad stepped in. "Here's the deal, Aaron. You don't want to go to this camp? Then we're going to our own wilderness survival camp. Just you and me."

"Dad! I wouldn't go with you to Disney World! You can't control me! You two are always trying to control me!"

"Stop it! Both of you!" Mom jumped up from the kitchen table.

"Unless you two can work something out, and real soon, you, sweetheart, are going to Montana. I'm sorry. You know I love you. We love you, but . . . ." She started to cry. Dad hugged her. I felt bad for Mom, but there was no way I was going off to some camp with guards and barbed wire.

Then Dad e-mailed this place he'd heard about from our friends Roger and his daughter, Lisa. Bowron Lakes Provincial Park. Way up in British Columbia, not too far from where we'd gone island-hopping in sea kayaks last year, starting in Bella Bella. Bowron Lakes is a seventy-two-mile round-trip chain of lakes in the Cariboo Mountains, which parallel the Canadian Rockies to the east. Dad made reservations to put in a kayak on May 15. First day of the season.

Then this amazing thing happened. Dad met with Mr. Hyde, the principal, and Ms. Dunn, my English teacher, and worked out a deal. Instead of getting expelled, I got suspended for two weeks. And here's where my English teacher comes in: for missing two weeks of school, I agreed to keep a journal, then shape it into a story. With characters, problems, a climax, and some kind of resolution.

Or fail to graduate from middle school.

I complained to Ms. Dunn, "But I don't know *how* to write a story!"

She nodded, "When you're about to begin a story and you're staring at that blank page and then you start writing, it can feel like leaping off a mountain . . . or plunging down a waterfall in a tiny kayak." This image made her smile.

I don't know why, but when she said "leaping off a mountain," GRIZZLY PEAK popped into my mind. Maybe a title for my story?

But I didn't have a story.

"You might not know where you're going," she continued, "but you keep going until you come to the end. Stories have a beginning, a middle, and an end."

Through this big writing lecture I'm thinking one thing: *Sweet!* No school for two weeks! Kayaking and camping out in a mountain wilderness. Roasting marshmallows over an open fire. And fresh-caught fish!

Then I think: *Wait!* Two weeks with Dad! Just the two of us. Three days in the car—*each way!*—with him listening to old-time jazz or classical music. And he'd already warned me: "No electronics, Aaron. No cell phone, no texting, no Facebook or Twitter or Instagram. No iPod."

We fought back and forth.

Finally, I said, "Okay! I'll go. But *only* if I can listen to my iPod in the car. I won't take it kayaking. Just in the car."

He had to think about that for a while.

Finally he agreed. "*Deal.* Now are we good to go?" He wanted to bump my fist, all buddy-buddy, but I turned away.

But the trip was a *go!* Somehow I'd have to survive two weeks alone with my dad, *and* become a writer!

ALL THE
WAYS TO DIE

Okay, let's zoom ahead. The next three days we drove—from our house near the coast in Northern California, clear up through the Northwest, across the border, and into western Canada. I didn't talk to my dad and he didn't talk to me. I listened to Macklemore and Jay Z and Eminem on my iPod and he listened to Frank Sinatra and Tony Bennett and Miles Davis.

He'd go to bed early and I spent the late hours catching up on my journal. I was actually starting to enjoy it. The writing I mean. And I have to admit I was beginning to get psyched about our kayak trip. Another adventure! A scarier adventure though, because it would be my first time ever *river* kayaking.

Only I wished I were going with my buddies Roger and Lisa and Cassidy instead of my dad. We drove within sixty miles of Roger and Lisa's house in Oregon, but he wouldn't stop and visit. No matter how much I begged him. Lisa and I follow each other on Twitter and Instagram, but I couldn't wait to see her again. In the flesh.

Now it's late in the morning of May 15. We've been on the road two and a half days—ten or eleven hours each of the first two days, and we got up just after dawn this morning to get here before noon.

Finally, we rattle down the clattering gravel road to this remote outpost of civilization. Bowron Lakes Provincial Park. Four hundred and fifty miles north of the US border. Eleven lakes—linked in places by rivers and streams—carving a rectangular circuit through the glacial Cariboo Mountains of central British Columbia.

You can Google it. But you can't know how it *feels* to be here.

It's complicated. I'll try to explain it.

I'm impatient to get going, and yet I've never done any river kayaking before. I was great at sea kayaking by the end of our Bella Bella trip last summer. And pretty good going down the Green River through Desolation Canyon, but that was in a rubber raft.

Now we're heading off on a seventy-two-mile *river* kayak trip through the Canadian wilderness. As I learned rafting the Green River, rivers can have rapids and tight curves and waterfalls. It's a totally different thing from sea kayaking. Trust me.

While Dad's signing in and getting permits and maps at the visitor's center, he's left me to haul the kayak off the roof by myself. And to get all our gear together. Already he's giving me all the work.

And the kayak is a monster. Seventeen feet long! It's really a "tracking" or lake kayak, with a rudder that you can drop in—to help you going straight ahead—or pull out when you don't need it. It's not near as sleek and light as a real *river* kayak. And it doesn't have a pedal-and-cable operated rudder that swivels, like the sea kayaks we used, island-hopping off Bella Bella last summer.

But I look around and I've got to admit: it's beautiful here. Totally. Snowcapped peaks everywhere. You can inhale the scent of pine trees and feel the hugeness of the wilderness here. Last night we saw three wolves leaping across the road in front of our car. That image will burn in my memory forever.

And now I hear what sounds a little like a wolf. But I know from our Bella Bella trip, it's the crazy yodeling call of a loon.

I look up. The sun is playing peekaboo with the clouds. There's no way to know which way this day will go. We're in the mountains. The weather could flip like a coin. It could be smooth sailing under the sun. Or misery under a cold, crashing rain.

That's how it feels. It feels like the unknown. And I love it and fear it at the same time.

But I'm not going to show it. To show it is to open myself up to my dad. And that can be dangerous. For both of us.

So when Dad comes walking toward me with a big smile on his face, I don't smile back. I wipe the cold sweat from my face to let him know how hard I've been working.

"Good news!" he says. "The season has just opened and so far we're the only ones who've signed in. The *first* ones, Aaron! How cool is *that?* The ranger said the snows here were pretty heavy this winter, so the rivers are up and moving fast. That's good, but could be scary too. It's gonna be a real challenge, Aaron, but that's why we're here."

You're the challenge, I want to say. And I'm here because I got kicked out of school for no real reason, and you made me come. But it beats going to a locked down camp in Montana.

But whatever.

I start pulling more stuff out of our car when a ranger comes out of the station toward me. She's tall and totally gorgeous and when she smiles my insides soften. She looks around eighteen but is probably a lot older, and has freckles and long red hair and when the wind blows her hair across her eyes she reminds me, just a little—just for a moment—of Lisa.

"Welcome to Bowron Lakes!" she says. "You'll be the first ones in this season. You'll have the whole wonderful wilderness to yourselves. But I hope you've had some experience. The snow in the mountains is melting and the rivers are high. The forecast shows high winds and thunderstorms, which can turn to snow flurries this time of year. Wind can cause standing waves on these lakes. That can be a real hazard, as I guess you know. Best to get going while the going's good!"

"Um, thanks." I want to say something clever but I can't think of a single clever thing to say. Why am I suddenly so tongue-tied and shy?

"Aaron!" Dad calls from the far side of the car. "Let's boogie!"

Geez, Dad! I'm thinking. Do you have to say *boogie?*

"Have an awesome trip!" the ranger says.

I'm already turning away and I give her the thumbs up without turning around.

Dad's stuffing wet bags into the fore (or forward) cargo hold of our kayak. I start stuffing gear into the aft (or stern or rear) cargo hold.

We loaded up with food for a little over a week at a supermarket back in Seattle. Lots of canned goods and freeze-dried and pepperoni sticks and gorp. Everything goes into these rubber "wet bags" that you roll up at the top and snap shut to keep watertight. So why aren't they called "dry bags?" Random!

"You better stuff your sleeping bag at the *bottom* of the wet bag, Aaron, not the top," my father says. "In case water leaks in." (Yeah, like it did when I capsized on our Bella Bella trip.)

"I'm not about to repack the whole bag, Dad."

"Okay," he says. "It's *your* sleeping bag." Scowl scowl.

"Dude! Why are you always all up in my face?" I click the bag shut and cram it into the hold.

"Where's the coffee, Aaron? We can't forget the coffee."

I just shrug. He can't live without his coffee.

Actually I like caffeine too. Who doesn't? But he gets so hyper just talking about it.

Finally, he finds the coffee and we give our station wagon a once over and decide that we haven't forgotten anything.

He locks the car and then claps his hands together and says, "Okay, Aaron. Let's boogaloo down Broadway!"

"*Geez!* Do you always have to talk like a moron? It's embarrassing!"

"So who's to hear it?" He makes a mock search, left and right.

"I am! I wish I wasn't!"

"Okay, then. Let's roll, *fool!* Is that better, *dawg?*"

I roll my eyes. "You're such a loser," I say under my breath.

"So lift, Aaron. I got this end, you got that end. We have

a mile and a half portage to Kibbee Lake. That's where we put in."

"*Whaaat?* You're trippin' if you think I'm carrying this loaded kayak to the next lake! It must weigh like two hundred pounds! Didn't you see the sign back there to rent portage carts? You know, those carts with wheels? You put the kayak on it and roll. *Dude!*"

"I'm not renting one of those, Aaron! We have arms and legs. We don't need a *portage* cart." He pronounces it the French way, pour-tahzh, which gets an eye roll from me.

"Now I said 'lift!' So *lift!*"

"We have arms and legs so why do we drive a car, Dad? This is the twenty-first century. They have wheels now. Wheels roll. They're cool."

"Actually," comes a woman's voice off to the side, "Aaron's probably right." It's the gorgeous park ranger. She's got a ranger's jacket on now and she's standing next to a gravel-dinged Ford pickup.

"Without a cart, if one of you gets injured you're just plain stuck. And you don't want to be stuck out there, especially this time of year. This is grizzly country. Few people, but a whole lot of hungry grizzlies. And moose with calves. Mama moose. They're even more dangerous. And with the rivers up right now, it's tricky. We had lots of accidents last year. Lots of canoes lost. And an eleven-year-old Boy Scout lost his life."

Geez! I want to ask her how but Dad cuts me off.

"In the old days trappers portaged without the help of carts," he says. All of a sudden he's Macho Man. And he hates macho men. Go figure.

"But I guess you're right, Miss . . . uh . . . Ms. . . ."

"Just call me Pam." She beams and reaches out and shakes his hand.

Then she bumps my fist with her freckled fist. "You keep your daddy in line, Aaron!"

We both laugh. It's my first laugh in a long time. She's pretty chill. Pretty *and* chill.

"Tell ya what," she says. "Just take that portage cart over there. You can fold it and secure it to your kayak for when you need it. No rental fee required, okay? But you'd better bring it back. It's my hide if you don't!"

"It's probably ours too," Dad says, without smiling.

But for once he's probably right

How did that Boy Scout die? I wonder.

Drowned?

Clawed by a grizzly?

Mauled by a moose?

Attacked by a mountain lion?

Fell off a cliff and broke his neck?

I think of all the ways to die in the wilderness.

It makes me shiver.

And as we slide the kayak onto the two-wheeled cart and wave good-bye, I feel, for the first time, the sharp talons of anxiety.

THE DAY A GRIZZLY ATE MY DAD

We take turns pulling the portage cart. When one pulls the other pushes. I don't know which I hate more. It's harder to pull but you have to walk bent over when you push. It makes me feel like an old man. But either way, it beats carrying the kayak—packed with all our gear—on our shoulders.

One good thing is there are no mosquitoes. Maybe because it's too early in the season, or because of the wind. Or maybe just because it's midday and sunny, and they're going to pour out and swarm us and eat us alive at dusk.

Even though the wind's blowing down off the snowy peaks, it's getting warm and I'm sweating. I just want to be on the lake, gliding along.

Or up in that snow, on one of those mountains.

I look up. I wonder if one of them is actually called Grizzly Peak.

I almost stumble. I look back at the ground to watch where I'm going.

It's bumpy but pretty flat. The tree branches—mostly red cedar like we'd seen island-hopping last year—reach out and scratch our arms at times, but otherwise (I have to admit) it's an awesome stretch.

I look up now and then and there's always these beautiful mountains in the distance. Still, I keep my eyes open for grizzly bears and moose.

But all I see is a golden marmot bumbling through the scrub, a red squirrel, and a few northern jays darting from tree to tree, jabbering like pirates.

But I do see the deep tracks of what's got to be a moose alongside the gravel path. Huge cleft hoofprints, like giant deer tracks, in the mud. When my dad points them out I just shrug, but they're really pretty cool. There's signs of life out there. Something bigger than us, and far from our everyday lives.

Suddenly dark clouds start rolling in, burying the sun. At least that gives us a little break from the growing heat, but not much.

When we finally get to Kibbee Lake I want to strip down and jump in and swim. But I don't. The water's too cold. I kneel down and splash the glacial melt onto my face. It's like being slapped by hands of ice.

I stand up and breathe in. If I could breathe in the whole lake and not drown, I would.

We're here! I want to shout. *We're finally HERE!*

When Dad says, "We're here, Aaron!" it's like an echo of my mind.

I pull my paddle out of the cockpit and say, "Let's roll!"

"Hold your horses," Dad says, getting all folksy now that we're out in the wilderness. "We have to secure the cart to the kayak. Maybe we should have a snack first. We may regret it if we don't."

Dad folds the handle and bungee-cords the cart to the bow of the kayak, then starts opening the forward hold. I'm hungry but I just want to get going.

"Why don't we snack later?" I say. "Can't we keep going?"

Dad scratches the stubble on his face. "Okay. You sit in front. I'll steer." Here we go again. On our Bella Bella trip, I had to earn that position in back, where you have more control of the kayak, before he'd let me sit there. As always, Dad wants to control everything. Whatever. I just want to get moving.

He starts shoving the kayak into the shallows. I help.

"Wait," he says. "We better put on our spray skirts. Looks like rain."

Right on cue the wind picks up and there's a roll of thunder. **Ka-BOOM!** Sounds like the gods bowling in the mountains. A jagged branch of lightning lights up the insides of a cloud.

"Sorry, Aaron. Can't go out on the lake if there's lightning!"

I know he's right but I can't wait. I just stand there. A gust of wind almost knocks me over.

"We can't do it," he says. "We'll be the tallest thing on the lake. A magnet to lightning. We'll have to wait and see which way the storm goes."

It's so frustrating, I throw my double-bladed paddle like a spear. It skims along the shallows, starts to sink, and bobs back up. It floats in a slow spiral into some reeds, not far from shore.

"You can't control your anger any more than you can control the weather, can you?" Dad says. He pulls the kayak back up the muddy incline.

He's right. But it's hard to admit. It's like everything's conspiring to shut this trip down just when I really want it to take off.

The first drops pock the surface of the water as I wade in, wearing my river sandals, and snatch up my paddle before it drifts away.

I squelch back out and stand under a short tree, leaning against the rough trunk. "Sorry," I mumble.

The drops are flying sideways now in the wind, like stinging needles of ice. Dad tosses me a poncho from a wet bag and puts one on. He hauls the kayak in under some branches. He's skinny but strong. Tallish, all bones. But his bones must be attached by steel cable.

I wrestle into my poncho and slide down the tree trunk to my heels, before the wind can blow me down. Great start, I think. Just great. Black clouds boiling and **Ka-BOOM**! The dark sky lights up with an electrical charge and goes dark again.

But the next flash of lightning is farther away. I count the seconds till the thunder booms. At least three miles away. I can still see lightning dancing on the peaks, but it's moving on.

And except for the wind, the storm is gone as quick as it had begun.

"Give me a hand here." Dad starts pulling the kayak back down toward the water. I shuffle after him and push. My jeans are soaked up to my crotch, and my wet legs and feet are freezing cold.

But I don't care. I even take my poncho off. It just gets in the way. I just want to get going.

"First we better climb into our spray skirts," Dad says again, lowering the boat to the ground.

He fishes out his spray skirt from the leg space, steps

into it, and straps it on over his shoulders. He looks like a man in a skirt.

"I'll pass," I say.

"Then you'll learn the hard way. But don't bellyache to me that you're cold and wet when we're out on the lake. I'm not your mother."

If this was a movie and I had it on DVD, I'd skip forward to the fun part.

The Day a Grizzly Ate My Dad.

* * *

Dad's wearing river sandals and three-quarter-length pants. He wades in, pulling the prow rope with him. Then he swings the kayak sideways to the shore.

I step in and almost tip the boat. I know better. One leg flies out and I nearly topple over, but I catch myself and stand up in the murky muck, cursing.

A frog jumps and I could swear it's laughing at me.

I try again and this time I get myself seated. I'm out of practice and out of patience. We haven't been in a kayak for a year. Dad steps into the rear cockpit, squats, and sits down, all in one smooth, fast motion. He used to be the awkward one. Now I feel like the spaz.

Roger and Willie were the leaders on our last two trips. Now Dad wants to be the leader. But maybe I do too. Once I'm back in practice, that is.

He stretches the skirt and attaches the elastic hem to the

rim of his cockpit. Then he digs his paddle blade into the muck and starts pulling us out into the chop.

We paddle as hard as we can, but the wind hits the kayak and pushes the nose sideways and we start drifting rapidly backwards into the reeds. The wind lashes the surface of the lake, pushing water over our kayak.

I wish I was wearing my spray skirt. And my poncho too.

I hate it when Dad's right!

My paddle clashes with his. We're out of sync and spinning in circles. The boat rocks in the chop, water sloshing into my cockpit. In minutes I'm soaked to the skin.

I'm freezing. I mean I'm totally *freezing.* I'm wearing just a T-shirt and my arms are all goose-bumped. I'm shivering like a guy locked in a freezer and my teeth are clacking like dice.

Suddenly, standing waves start smacking us silly.

Dad's yelling and I'm almost in a rage of panic, but then into my head pops an image of me and Lisa in the sea kayak last year, waving our paddles around, laughing like loons.

As Dad yells some more, I can't help it: I laugh like a crazy person.

And then it happens.

We capsize.

FOOD FOR THE BEARS

Cold shock and darkness. Water everywhere. Pure instinct. Pushing free of the kayak. Following my bubbles toward the surface. Kicking, clawing, grasping for life.

Gasping for air. Lungs bursting.

Head blowing through the surface. Spluttering. Treading water. Wave in my mouth. Going back under.

Coming back up.

Alive! Alive! Alive!

Dad grabs me as I grab the kayak. It's bobbing upside down, two-thirds submerged. Awash in waves.

It's all total deja vu. Last year. Lisa and I capsizing in the riptide when it started flooding the lagoon. Hanging upside down. . . .

I kick my feet and hug the hull. Dad's beside me now, draped over the topsy-turvy boat like a dead otter.

My feet touch bottom. I get a purchase on it and lose it and get it again, heaving myself and the boat toward the shore.

We're not very far out. The wind and the waves slap at our backs and press us toward shore, through the chop, into the shallows, into the reeds.

Dad coughs and gags and then he's all adrenaline. Like me. Like a gorilla.

We heave and wrestle the heavy kayak back in, snatching at paddles, my poncho, Dad's water bottle glugging toward the bottom.

Grounded. The kayak's bottomed out. We squat and wait for the next wave to lift it up. And when it comes we lift with a burst of energy and flip the boat.

Right-side up. It floats for a moment and we slide it up on shore. Then we collapse in the mud like puppets with our strings cut.

We look at each other. And I almost laugh again.

* * *

The squall is gone. The wind has died. The sun tiptoes out like a blazing ballerina and makes a grand stage entrance between the drifting clouds.

We've rocked the water out of the cockpits. The hatch covers and sealed bulkheads have kept the cargo holds almost watertight. And the wet bags have done their job. We've opened and checked them all. They're spread out on the mud like beached seals.

We're exhausted. We're shipwrecked sailors lying next to them, soaking in the rays of the sun.

We've stripped and put on dry clothes. Our wet clothes, squeezed and hung, drip from low hanging branches. Our shirts fill with ghosts of wind.

We're not speaking. I've been wavering between hilarity and horror. Relief and anger.

Anger at my dad. Anger at myself.

This shouldn't have happened.

This *did* happen.

Why?

I don't know.

I know it's not all Dad's fault, but I wish it was.

* * *

Finally, he rouses himself. "We can't stay here," he says, rising to one elbow. "We'll camp at the first campsite we come to."

"Why can't we just camp here? I'm starving!"

"We have to stay in a designated campsite. That's the rule. And like the ranger said, we're in grizzly country. There are bear caches at the campsites. We don't want to lose all our food on our first night out, right?"

"I haven't seen a single bear, Dad."

"That doesn't mean they're not here."

Suddenly, I feel the eyes of a hundred grizzlies on me. A hundred hungry bears. I roll over and groan. I get on all fours. I feel like a bear. A hungry bear.

I ROAR!

It sounds more like a croak and it's kind of funny, but Dad's not going for it.

"Why don't you laugh, Dad?" I sit up, wipe mud from my elbows with the edge of my towel.

"Is something funny, Aaron?"

"Everything's funny. You. Me. Man, we capsized within *three minutes* of taking off! That's pretty funny, don't ya think?"

"It was my fault," he says grimly. Where's this guy's sense of humor? "I let you rush me. We should've stopped and eaten before we hit the water. We should've waited to see which way the storm went. I should've made you wear your spray skirt. Water filled your cockpit and destabilized the boat. It was my fault."

My laughter flees like autumn leaves. Dad has a funny way of saying it's *his* fault.

I smack the ground and jump up.

"What you mean is it's *my* fault. Right, Dad?"

"Aaron, listen. You're not listening to me! I took off work just so you and I could do this. You could've had your 'wilderness survival experience' in Montana, but I wanted you to have it here. With me. No guards. No barbed wire. Just you and me. This is for *you*, Aaron. Someday you'll understand that."

There's nothing I can say to that. I suppose he's right. But I just can't admit that.

Not yet. Maybe someday, but not now. Not yet.

Right now all I can think is: He has a backhanded way of blaming me while *claiming* the fault is his.

Maybe someday he'll see *that*.

* * *

I slap the first mosquito of the trip. The sun's going down beyond the snowy peaks. We're in the cold shadows of the Cariboo Mountains.

Another mosquito buzzes and whines and I slap it away. We've snacked and loaded the kayaks again and we're about to launch for the second time on our maiden voyage.

This time I use my spray skirt. And put on my poncho.

I may learn the hard way, but at least it's *my* way.

* * *

There's still enough daylight to see by. Just. The lake is as flat and reflective as a mirror now, and when we push off it feels like we're sliding on ice.

I've talked Dad into letting me sit in the stern and steer. I told him if he wants me to build up my "self-confidence," like he claims, there's no better way to do it.

"That's your counselor who cares about your self-confidence. But I'm fine with that, Aaron. He's right and you're right. Go for it."

This time I *know* I'm right.

And it feels good.

We leave the mosquitoes behind. Water drips down my

arms from the paddle, but the rest of me stays dry. For a while we follow a couple of loons. Sometimes we get close enough to see the red of their eyes. Whenever we get too close they dive down and we never know where they'll bob back up.

The sky's washed clean now of clouds and the mountains are getting closer and higher. Tall cedars wave from shore in the slight breeze and the ripple of the paddles in the water is the only sound.

By the time we reach the campsite it's twilight. A fingernail moon dangles in the notch between peaks, about to set. We haven't seen a soul all day. There's no wind now but the

mosquitoes on land aren't so bad. Too cold for mosquitoes, I'm thinking. Lucky us.

I rub my shoulders. They ache. Long time since I've paddled like that. But I did get the hang of it quickly again, which I'm proud of, and after the fiasco of the first launch, my paddle only clacked with Dad's once or twice.

We were in sync.

"Let's set up camp before it's too dark," he says.

We pitch a two-man mountain tent even though I'd wanted my own tent. But Dad had said that two tents would weigh too much and take up too much space in the kayak.

We set up a rainfly over the tent and over the fire ring,

because the sky looks threatening again. Firewood's provided at this campsite but I search for bigger chunks of deadwood, and scare up some creature that bursts away into low brush. A fox, I think. Or a lynx. I'd love to see a lynx!

Eventually we get a pretty good fire going in the fire ring.

We eat canned beans with bacon bits, and out here it tastes great. I'm so hungry I could eat all the beans myself—*and the can!*

The moon's down now and the stars are crowding in. I just want to lie back and gaze up at the stars, but Dad says we have to clean up. Can't leave food for the bears. Even the garbage. We'll have to pack the garbage out, but meanwhile we store it with the food in the bear locker. A metal box with a sunken handle only humans can open (hopefully).

After washing the dishes, I lie back on the bank. I listen to the water lapping and the night sounds and watch the stars. It's so clear now that the Milky Way pours across the night like spilled cream.

Dad sits beside me. "What do you think?" he says. "About all this?"

"Not too bad." It's hard to admit, but it's really pretty cool being here.

Epic even.

"This is what it's all about," he says. "There's beauty and there's terror in the world, Aaron. I saw nights like this in the desert, when I was in Iraq during the war."

"Why don't you ever talk about it, Dad? I mean, going

over there and fighting and stuff. Were you afraid? Did you kill anyone? You've never told me anything about it."

He doesn't answer for a while. Finally, he says, "Not right now, Aaron. We're here now and I just want to enjoy it." He tosses a pebble into the lake and watches it sink. "Time to hit the hay." He climbs to his feet and wanders off toward the tent.

Beauty and terror. Sounds like something he told me when we were on that wild trip down through Desolation Canyon, two long years ago.

I've come a long way since then, I think.

Then again, maybe not far enough.

I stare at the fire. The flames dance like devilish creatures in the night.

* * *

Later, when I join him in the tent, he's already snoring. I lie awake, listening to the forest. The wind's picking up again, to a dull roar. It makes me think of grizzlies out there.

I hear a branch snap. Near our tent.

A grizzly. *I'm sure of it!* Prowling for food.

I think of waking Dad, but I don't. What could he do? I shrink into myself. Pull my bag up over my head. As if that will do any good against a hungry grizzly.

It's the end of Day One. We have six days to go.

If we live that long.

THE VISITOR AND THE LUNATIC MOOSE

In the morning we see bear tracks in the mud. All through our camp. Huge, deep prints, with five toes and sharp claw marks. I was right!

"Grizzly," Dad declares. "Check out the size of the tracks."

I think of the lost Boy Scout and a shiver runs through me.

We start building a fire for cooking, looking around every few seconds for last night's visitor.

It's warmer today, and swarms of mosquitoes emerge from the shadows. They buzz and whine. We swat and yell—as if yelling will do any good—and race back to the tent. Dad gets out the bug spray. He pulls off his shirt and shrouds himself in a mist of repellent. Then hands it to me.

I wonder if it would repel grizzlies, too. Take *that! Pssst! Pssssssssst!*

When the sun strikes our camp and the breeze picks up, the mosquitoes fade away and we get breakfast going. Dad fries eggs and bacon and boils coffee, while I use a small hand pump to filter the lake water, so I can fill our water bottles for the day.

The bacon's burnt but I like it that way. There's no milk for the coffee but I drink it anyway, with lots and lots of sugar, while I look at the map.

"Aaron!" Dad claps his hands together. "We've got to get this camp shipshape, and weigh anchor. *Pronto!*"

"Geez, Dad! You sound like Roger and Willie, all rolled into one!" Roger with his pirate talk. Willie with his cowboy drawl.

He snaps me with a towel. I grab it and almost pull him into the fire.

He almost laughs. Not quite.

"Seriously," he says, all business now. As usual. "Our little spill lost us a day yesterday. We should've made it across Indian Point Lake by last night. And we have a long uphill portage just to get there. And that's *after* we paddle across the rest of Kibbee Lake!"

The day's just begun and he's already barking orders at me.

"I'll take care of the tent," he says. "You do the dishes and douse the fire. And be sure to scrub the frying pan good."

"How about I take down the tent and *you* scrub the frying pan?"

He folds his arms across his chest and glares at me.

"Fine!" I grab the pan and a pot, plus my dishes, and head down to the water. Actually I like dousing the fire.

I like the way it sizzles and steams up. I like to watch the last embers shrivel and die. *Pzzzzzzzzz.*

We're back out on the lake within the hour. I'm in the stern again. I release the rudder line by hand so the rudder plops in, because we're making a beeline for the far end of the lake and a strong breeze is shoving us sideways.

There are small waves but we slice right through them. I love being low in the water. In a canoe you sit well above the surface, but in a kayak you feel like you're inside the water, a part of the boat.

We get into a rhythm. We both paddle with strong, smooth strokes, and never clash. We're totally synchronized now.

If only our lives we're in sync like this, Dad and I would be models of the perfect father and son.

But we're not. Not in sync. And not models.

And yet, while we're plowing through the waves, I get a glimpse of how it could be.

And I don't hate it.

* * *

No more sign of bear. No movement on shore. No wind. No waves. All is still and silent, except for the soft, steady paddle-splashes we make as we glide across the pure mirror reflection of the sky.

* * *

Kibbee Lake "accomplished" (Dad lingo), an hour later and we're portaging the 1.2 miles to Indian Point Lake. Even with the cart it's hard work. We don't speak. We sweat.

To forget the pain, I let my mind wander. I wonder who the Indians were here, or the First Nations people, as they're called in Canada. And if there are any still around here. I wonder if they made dugout or birch bark canoes, and if they portaged them upside down, on their shoulders with their heads inside. Or if they used a travois to drag them along the ground.

I bet they wished they had portage carts like we have, and I'm glad that Pam, the pretty park ranger, talked Dad into using one.

Small birds flit and flicker between the trees, chipmunks chuckle, and sweat drips down my sides. The sun's straight up and there's no shade. We're trudging steadily uphill. My legs feel like lead pipes.

When we finally arrive at Indian Point Lake—which tapers at the far end and looks calm at the moment—we plop down on the shore and eat a snack of gorp and guzzle filtered water. I gobble two energy bars.

As we sit there, everything changes. I can feel it. It's ominous. A huge dark cloud blocks the sun now. A cool breeze slides down from the mountains and makes me shiver.

Out on the lake the sky continues to darken. No big thunderclouds, just a solid gray, like the underbelly of a whale.

Dad doesn't need to say, *Put on your spray skirt, Aaron. It looks like rain.*

I put on my spray skirt all on my own, wash down the energy bars, and we're ready to push off. Me in the back again. The boat at my command.

By the time we're halfway down the length of Indian Point Lake, it begins to rain. A light, steady rain. Since I have my spray skirt on, attached to my cockpit, I have to release it to grab my poncho, which I keep tucked behind my back as a kind of cushion.

While I do that, we start drifting with the wind. "Stay on course!" Dad snaps, yelling over his shoulder.

"I'm putting on my poncho!" I yell back. "Calm down."

While Dad gets into his poncho, I use my paddle to adjust our direction, lining up the bow with the tallest tree at the end of the lake. Soon we're a team of two again.

Barely.

That's when I see something along the shore. It's dark brown, and it's large. From here I can't tell if it's a moose or a grizzly bear, but—from the safety of our kayak—I aim to find out.

I pull up the rudder so I can change course and stroke wide on the right side till the nose swings around toward the left, and we begin heading toward whatever it is.

"Aaron! What the—"

"There's a moose or a bear, Dad! Over there against the shore. I want to see it. Okay?"

Dad wants to see it, too—whatever it is—as much as I do. I can tell by his posture.

As we get closer it gets bigger. And then we know what it is.

"Bull moose!" Dad yells. Nuzzling the lake water, Moose stands up to his knees in the sedge grass sprouting from the shallows.

He's a hundred yards away.

Seventy-five.

Fifty.

He lifts his great flat rack up and water pours off like miniature waterfalls from his antlers and the duckweed in his mouth. He keeps chewing, chewing, watching us with beady eyes.

I paddle harder toward shore, into the duckweed, as Dad yells, "Hold up, Aaron! Not too close!"

But I keep paddling.

Dad back-paddles just as hard—*away* from the moose.

It's a standoff.

"Aaron!"

"I'm not going to run him over, Dad! I just want to see him better."

"He's gonna run us over if we get any closer, Aaron! Moose can be more dangerous than bears! Unpredictable!"

"*Chill,* Dad! We're not hurting the moose, and he's not going to hurt us!"

"I told you to back off, Aaron! Listen to me! I'm telling you!"

You're trying to control me again, but I don't say it. I keep paddling.

We're still far enough away from the moose. It's not like they can swim, after all.

I'm wrong! Suddenly the huge bull moose comes crashing toward us. In no time he's swimming, and he's swimming fast: knees working like pistons, hooves churning, nostrils flaring.

And all of a sudden I'm back-paddling with Dad. I plunge the blade in the water near the stern and we pivot on a dime. Then we forward paddle so fast we churn the water with our blades like a paddleboat.

Away from the moose.

"Paddle, Aaron! Paddle!"

"Paddle, Dad! *Harder!*"

I glance over my shoulder. The moose is just a paddle length behind us! He's snorting like a demonic horse, snot flying out of his huge nostrils. We had trampled his duck-weed . . .

. . . and now he's gonna trample *us!*

OKAY, TARZAN

But just as I decide that we're about to be capsized by a lunatic moose, the beast changes his mind and swims a wide circle back toward shore, still chugging like a steam engine.

We're still flying along, skimming the waves, riding on the jet fuel of terror.

Good-bye, Moose!

I want to holler and cheer. I raise my paddle with both hands above my head and yodel like Tarzan.

A loon yodels back.

Or maybe it's a wolf. I can feel my blood coursing through my veins and my nerves singing like a steel guitar. We're *rockin'!*

But my dad, he stops paddling. His head's down and his shoulders are hunched.

Here it comes. I know it's coming.

But it doesn't. He just shakes his head, face down, and takes a deep breath. A long, loud breath. In, then out.

While Dad gives me the silent treatment, I keep paddling. I want to enjoy this small victory. Maybe it was dumb, racing toward a moose, but it feels heroic. Epic! Super fantastic!

* * *

After awhile Dad starts paddling with me, and we get back into our rhythm again. The rain lightens, almost goes away, comes back. Turns into a hard, pounding rain. Then silence.

The birds are hiding. I look for moose. I look for bear.

Nothing. Just dense green forest all around. Mountains sweeping up into clouds. The sky crouching down on us, ready to pounce.

I want more action. I want another moose—or better yet a grizzly—breathing down my back.

Is that sick or what? I don't know. All I know is that it makes me feel something. Something other than mad.

I wish Lisa were here, with her smile and sparkling eyes. Even Cassidy. Bad boy Cassidy. He would've loved that moose!

Of course, he probably would've raced toward it first and stole all my thunder.

Whatever. I miss them both. Especially when Dad's giving me the silent treatment. Again.

I hunker down, and let the slow rain fall.

* * *

Near the end, Indian Point Lake grows narrower and narrower, and finally meanders through a small marsh dotted with beaver dams and lodges.

The drizzle has stopped. I look around for a beaver, and sure enough I spot a V-shaped wake trailing silently behind a furry head. It's maybe fifteen yards away, heading for a lodge. I tap Dad's back and point.

We both stop paddling, and stay absolutely still, practically holding our breath.

And for a while the beaver glides with us, at one point getting within five feet of our bow. It's as if we're floating in a bubble where time stands still.

But then Dad starts paddling again and breaks the bubble. The beaver slaps its tail, and goes under.

Dad's still upset about the moose. I can feel it.

The clouds are retreating but the sky darkens toward twilight. My stomach growls. I've got to eat.

I'm starving and the high of the moose encounter has drained out of me. And after hours of paddling I'm just dog-tired. Beat. Bushed.

How will I finish paddling to the end of the lake, let alone have the energy to set up camp. Make a fire. Eat. And write in my journal.

When we do finally reach the end of Indian Point Lake, I drive our kayak hard and fast through the shallows and thrust the bow right up onto land. But it takes the very last ounce of my strength.

That's when Dad steps out of the kayak, straightens up, and says, "Okay, Tarzan. Now it's time for the portage to Isaac Lake."

WHERE THE WILD THINGS ARE

Dad bends over and starts pulling the kayak further out of the water just as I'm stepping out. I lose my balance and fall flat on my face in the mud.

I slap the mud, rise to my knees, and stand up.

"*Thanks,* Dad." I swipe mud from my face and flick it into the water.

"Sorry, Aaron. My bad."

"Don't say 'my bad!' You sound like a moron!"

Dad ignores this, but now we're even. After all, he made me fall in the mud. I know it was an accident, but still. . . .

Dad releases the bungee cords holding the portage cart and sets it up.

"We have to portage to Isaac Lake, Aaron. This isn't a good place to camp. It's way too marshy. Sure to be a breeding ground for mosquitoes."

As if to make his point, a mosquito bites my neck. I slap it, leaving a smear of blood on my palm about the size of a quarter.

I'm in no mood for mosquitos. I feel a brief jolt of energy out of sheer anger. Anger about the unexpected portage and Dad making me fall in the mud.

What happened to the quiet magic with the beaver?

* * *

The portage is 1.6 kilometers. About a mile. I'm so beyond tired it's like walking in a dream. A *bad* dream, plagued by mosquitoes.

By the time we set up camp, the drizzle has started and stopped again, and it's almost full dark. Dad has lit a lantern. The clouds are breaking up and stars start popping out, one by one. The moon is low, shrouded by a cloud.

We make a fire, cook a freeze-dried chicken dinner, eat, and clean up, without saying a word. Then we sit back and watch the flames licking the night. You could cut the silence between us with a knife.

Sometimes I feel like we're an old married couple.

I want a divorce!

I almost chuckle at that thought, but I don't.

I look up at the descending moon, larger than yesterday's, burning just above the peaks to the west.

Is Lisa looking at the same moon?

A chilly breeze with the smell of snow on it has chased away the mosquitoes. I scoot closer to the fire.

I realize I feel proud, in a way. We've completed our first

full day of paddling. We've covered a lot of miles today, more than making up for yesterday.

It should be a night for drinking hot cocoa and roasting marshmallows. But Dad's still not speaking, and the tension between us keeps building.

I'm starting to feel like a tea kettle about to blow when Dad finally breaks the silence. "Okay, Aaron. Got to get an early start tomorrow. We're doing Isaac Lake. It's twenty-three miles long, the longest lake in the circuit."

"Tell me we're not doing it in one day. We're not, right?"

"Wrong. I want to do it in a day. It'll be a good challenge. If you can make it tomorrow . . . well, that would be a great achievement, wouldn't it?"

"Geez! What is this? *A test?*"

A small house of fire collapses, sending spark-filled smoke up to the stars.

"A challenge. Like I said, this is why we're here, Aaron."

"What? You think you're building up my confidence by constantly whittling it away?"

"Only *you* can build your self-confidence, Aaron. Nobody can do it for you."

"Ha!" I say and jump up. I stomp off toward our tent, but then I keep going. I march straight into the night.

I crash through brush and trees and low-hanging branches. The stars are bright but the forest is dark. All I know is that I'm climbing steadily up—up what the map called Wolverine Mountain.

I wonder if there's a Grizzly Peak around here.

I pull my baseball cap down over my ears and pull up the hood of my hoodie, and walk hunched against a stiff, cold breeze flowing down the mountainside.

I trip. I fall. I get up.

I stumble over tree roots and small boulders and step into holes in the ground and keep going.

Suddenly I laugh for no reason and start to run wildly, uphill. Always uphill.

Before, I was exhausted, but now it's like I'm flying on a tank of coffee, a ton of sugar. It's a sugar high of insanity. I love it. I think I'll never go back.

I'll show *him* self-confidence. I'm almost drunk on it!

I jump up and swing from a branch and charge off through the night again. I can hear something crashing through the woods near me.

Probably just deer. But who knows? Maybe a wolverine? A grizzly?

Now I'm way up high above the star-freckled lake and I climb a huge boulder clinging to the steep slope of the mountain, and see the sharp claw of the moon as it plunges into darkness.

This is crazy mad fun, right?

It's so fun I start to howl. I howl like I did on the lake today. I howl and do a little dance on the top of the boulder and almost fall off, and laugh like a loon, and howl again.

And this time I *do* hear wolves. I'm sure of it. I heard one

on Vancouver Island last year, on our way home from Bella Bella.

And now, here I am, all alone, howling, and the wolves are howling back at me! Sounds like there's a pack of them, off to the west, not far away. They make my blood sing, and I howl till my voice is as hoarse as a toad's.

Then I sit down on the boulder top and just listen. All around me the night has grown quiet. The wolves are silent now. Maybe they're watching me, yellow eyes lost among the trees. Maybe there are wolverines, too, watching, sniffing the night air.

Or grizzlies. Still as boulders, but for their fur, ruffled by the breeze.

I don't know. But I jump back up and do that little dance again, on the boulder top, and for a moment I am king. I am king of all the wild things, and all the wild things are awed into silence.

And I am awed into silence with them.

It's another epic moment, and I don't want it to end.

But then I hear my name being called: *"Aaaarrron! Aaaarrron!"*

I take a step backward—

—and suddenly I'm falling.

THE FREEDOM TO DIE

*B*AM!

    I land with a thud at the foot of the boulder. My shoulder takes the brunt of it, but then my head slams the ground. My mouth is filled with dirt.

And then my lights go out. All of them.

I don't know for how long.

And then I see stars and open my eyes.

Dad calls my name again. It's muffled by distance and a million trees. Or maybe there's something wrong with my ears now.

I climb to my feet and start stumbling back down the mountain, like a drunk bear. It's pitch-dark and fiercely cold and suddenly I feel all alone in the world. Lost and alone. And I don't know how I'll find my way back.

* * *

Next thing I know I'm waking up on the ground. My head

aches, my shoulder is killing me, and spears of sun pierce my eyes. I roll over.

Where am I?

I'm staring at a dead fire. I'm cold. I'm in my sleeping bag beneath a rainfly covered with dew. How did I get here?

I can't sit up. My eyes lift to an awesome sight. Mountains. The snow is down to maybe a thousand feet above us. Glacial water streams down in tiny cascades and rivulets. The sky above the peaks is a brilliant blue. There isn't a cloud anywhere. There isn't a trace of wind.

What happened last night?

I remember stumbling into trees and climbing a boulder and falling off the mountain and slamming my shoulder and my head. I remember being lost and not caring and laughing and then caring and not caring anymore.

A crow laughs from a branch. At least it sounds like laughter. Another crow cackles back from another tree. *Caw caw caw!*

Do the crows think I'm dead?

Am I dead but dreaming that I'm alive? Dreaming that I'm alive and awake?

I roll over and pain sears through my right shoulder like a blade of fire.

This is no dream! This is as real as it gets.

I remember a pain like this when I tried to land an ollie on my skateboard one time and slammed my shoulder into the sidewalk. Mom put ice on it.

Mom's a thousand miles away today.

But there *is* a freezing cold lake twenty feet away. I'm parched. And maybe it will help my aching head.

I sit up slowly and crawl over to the low bank. I lie on my belly and wiggle forward until I'm dangling above my reflection. Then I plunge my head into my reflection and shatter it.

Aaaaaargh! It's like shards of ice piercing my brain.

I gulp some freezing water and lift my head just as Dad comes running out of the tent. Water streams down my head and my face is probably turning blue.

Dad's mouth drops open. Then he starts to laugh, but holds it in and says, "You look like a drowned muskrat."

"I feel like a drowned muskrat . . . with a smashed shoulder." I almost laugh, too, but I hurt too much. Dad hands me a water bottle and I start glugging.

"Did you take a fall? You looked pretty banged up when you came staggering into camp last night. What happened?"

"Don't ask." I put down the bottle and pull off my hoodie. "I think I need ice for my shoulder."

"I think you need your head examined!" He squats down and looks at my bruised shoulder. "Ice would've helped last night. Too late now. And we have to get moving. Gotta get across this lake before the wind picks up. I read that Isaac Lake's notorious for its winds and sudden squalls."

"How can I paddle with this shoulder, Dad?"

"You should've thought of that when you went running

off into the dark last night. Moving it might actually help. Loosen it up. Get the circulation flowing."

I groan, pull off my T-shirt, then dip my shoulder into the icy cold water.

It doesn't help.

* * *

Dad turns on his heels and goes back to the tent, then returns and throws a small towel at my head. "Dry off. Get dressed. Let's get this show on the road!" Dad's no longer on the verge of laughter, and neither am I.

I don't feel like moving, but if I just lie here I'll freeze my butt off. And my stomach's growling with hunger.

And no, I don't want to stay here and become dinner for a hungry grizzly.

"Or dinner for you, ya hear me, Mr. Crow?" I actually yell at the crow, which almost makes me laugh again.

I towel off and start crawling toward my sleeping bag, but it hurts too much to crawl. I wobble to my feet and look down.

Crap! Where are my shoes?

* * *

Eventually, I find my river sandals in our tent. Turns out Dad had pulled them off me early this morning.

Now, out on the long narrow lake, it's so calm that the water seems part of the sky. We glide through it like a swan.

I'm up in front, in the fore cockpit as Dad calls it, and

this time I like it. I don't get to steer but I do get to set the pace. Dad has to synchronize his strokes to match mine. I started out paddling slow and ragged but now I'm going smoother and faster.

Don't tell Dad, but he was right. My shoulder hurt like hell when we started out, but now it's a dull ache lost in the immensity of this lake.

And I can rest if I want to while Dad paddles.

And I do. I scout the boulder-strewn shore for moose and bears, and spot a rare caribou.

Just a glimpse, frozen in place. Listening.

Then it gallops off into the tangle of woods.

I don't tell Dad. This is just for me.

I start paddling again and hear a high-pitched screech. I look up. A bald eagle soars above us. Its shadow slides over me. I speed up. It's a race.

We're soaring across the sky-lake when we hit a wall.

It's the wind. Dark clouds have been building up and now the squall hits the lake, turning the mirror surface into a cauldron of broken glass. We chop through the waves and soon my shoulder starts killing me again.

We're in the middle of the lake, far from shore. If we stop paddling, even for a moment, we'll drift backwards. So we keep paddling.

Now this is work.

And soon it feels like more than work.

It feels like survival. The sky's been steadily darkening and if rain joins this squall, we could be in trouble. On a lake this big—over twenty miles long—waves can get big, too. Like in the sea

And now I can smell rain on the wind.

If we get swamped out here by a standing wave, or capsized by the wind, there's nobody here to help us. And with my shoulder, swimming to shore would be a life or death matter.

We're on our own. Our lives are in our own hands.

I love it and hate it at the same time.

I hate it because it hurts. But I love it because if feels like *freedom!*

Though it could be the freedom to *die!*

And now I see the rain coming. It's like a swiftly moving doomsday shadow, a slanted wall of water.

And it's coming right for us.

THE BEAST
FOR REAL

When the wall of water hits us we're instantly soaked to the skin. There's no time to put on ponchos. We do have our spray skirts attached, which keep our lower bodies dry, but that's all.

The wind whips our kayak from side to side, but Dad holds the nose into the waves. If we get broadsided, that's it. We go over. In the middle of the lake.

A big lake. And we're far from shore.

The rain's so dense I can barely see the bow of the boat. It's like being inside an inferno of water. Dad's trying to yell over the roar. I can't hear what he's saying, but I think he's yelling, *"Paddle! Paddle!"*

What does he think I'm doing?

The bow rises and plunges and waves crash over us. Our paddles are "feathered" so the blades cut horizontally into the wind, but the paddle shudders in my hands and is almost ripped loose.

There's only one thing to do, and that is to hunker down

into the wind and paddle like demons.

Miraculously, the squall passes as suddenly as it struck. It's as if the rain gods have turned off a celestial spigot.

Thanks be to the rain gods!

The wind dies along with the squall. We rest our paddles across the hull and just float for a while. We're both breathing hard. We've earned a rest.

But a minute later Dad's back to being the king, the captain. "Okay, Aaron. If we're gonna make this whole lake while there's light, we've got to get paddling again."

"How about a lunch break, Dad?"

"Good idea." He tosses me a bag of gorp. It lofts over my shoulder and lands in my lap. "Chow down," he says. "You got two minutes."

I'm really getting ticked off, but somehow it doesn't touch me. The squall was like a cleansing. A trial by water. We've passed through it and we're as good as gold. The waves are flattening and I watch the sun dance silver dimes on the lake's surface, as I munch my gorp.

"Two minutes, Aaron!"

"Aye aye, sir!" I straighten up and salute my dad from the back of my head.

And I laugh to myself, thinking of Lisa again. Geez, if she were here now, we'd have the whole wilderness to ourselves! I'd bust a few rhymes for her, and maybe we'd dance to the stars, and watch the moon growing fat, like a piñata filled with candy.

Daydreaming like this, I paddle steadily and try to forget the pain in my shoulder. After a while I paddle on automatic, like the blades of a windmill. I churn through the water and I'm surprised Dad can keep up. He may be skinny and getting old, but it seems like he's getting tougher in his old age.

We keep up the furious pace and slide into one of the last campsites on the lake—after a whole day of paddling—just as the sun sinks behind the peaks.

"We did it, Aaron!" Dad crows. It's about as close to praise as I've gotten from him in a long time. It adds to the bubble of pride I feel rising to my heart, making it swell.

* * *

The bubble bursts while we're setting up camp. Every chore is murder. My right shoulder hurts again and I ache all over. But this time Dad filters the lake water while I build the fire. I make the best fires. And tonight we have an epic bonfire to celebrate today's legendary voyage. The flames leap up like crazy dancers at a late night concert.

And after dinner, for the first time, we *do* roast marshmallows and drink hot cocoa!

We're almost like a normal father and son enjoying a fun family vacation.

But I know it can't last.

And I'm right.

I make the mistake of mentioning Lisa. "So, I've been

thinking, Dad. Maybe we can swing by Roger and Lisa's on our way home?"

"I don't think so, Aaron." Dad slowly spins his sharpened stick and dips his marshmallow closer to the flames. "It's way out of our way. It's my responsibility to get you back to school by the end of May. And it's your responsibility to get with the schedule. You're supposed to be keeping a journal and writing a story. You have to keep up your end of the deal, kiddo."

"Like I'm not? I've been writing in my journal after you go to sleep. I've only missed one day! Cut me some slack."

"You've been getting too much slack, Aaron. That's the problem."

"Geez, Dad, it's too *close* not to make a little side trip to see them! Why do you have to be like this?"

Sometimes I feel like he's not really my father. That I'm adopted. That there's no way we share the same genes.

Suddenly, his marshmallow bursts into flame and he throws it and the stick it's on into the fire. "Sorry to spoil the party, Aaron, but tomorrow we do the Chute and the Roller Coaster. It's the only real white water of the trip, and from what I've read, it can be a boat graveyard for newbie paddlers."

He stands up and starts off toward our tent, then stops and turns around. "Don't forget to scrub the dishes and stash the food and garbage into the bear locker."

He sounds angry. Why does he sound angry?

He stares, then shakes his head. "I'm bushed, Aaron. I'm

calling it a night." He starts off again, but can't resist calling over his shoulder, "Don't forget! The bear locker!"

Just at that moment my marshmallow bursts into flame. But that's how I like it. I wave it like a torch in the night, then blow it out. I let it cool for a moment, then stick my teeth into the blackened crust and gooey white center.

Perfect.

I stay up late and roast and eat all the marshmallows in the bag. *All* of them! I eat until my teeth ache and my head aches and my belly's ready to burst.

My mouth and cheeks and hands get all sticky. I feel like shouting: *Forget the dishes. Forget the food. I'M the captain. I'M the King! Let the bears come! Let the grizzlies party!*

LET THE WILD RUMPUS BEGIN!

But I don't. I'm too responsible, even if my dad doesn't know it.

When I finally climb into our tent, next to my sleeping dad, I actually write LET THE WILD RUMPUS BEGIN! in my journal.

Then my pen slips from my fingers, and my eyes close.

* * *

It's nighttime but there's an otherworldly light shining and I'm skating down Wolverine Mountain—or is it Grizzly Peak?—my board rattling over stone. There's something big and hairy and scary right behind me, chasing me. A grizzly? But I don't care.

I'm swerving through trees, kick-flipping over logs, doing ollies over boulders, and catching a sky-full of air—and I'm free.

I'm *free!*

Snow glitters all around me and the cold bites my face but I'm flying. I am the wind and nothing can catch me.

But now I smell death. I smell the breath of the beast behind me—

And I jolt awake. I'm in the smelly tent. With Dad snoring and farting beside me.

There's a noise. Is that what woke me? A scratching. A chuffing. The sound of a beast digging, scraping . . . and it's right beside my ear!

My heart's crashing around again. I clutch myself in terror. Utter terror! I want to yell, to scream, but I have no voice. Not even a squeak.

Something nuzzles the door to the tent. There's an inward pressure pushing, pushing—until the whole tent begins to wobble.

Then a huge furry head bursts through!

THE BEAST ITSELF!

A GRIZZLY!

All fangs and claws. A massive explosion of violent gnashing.

Its great slobbering jaws open. . . .

I wake up. Again. There is no room for my heart. It is pounding like it will jump out of my chest. There is

certainly no more room for bad dreams.

I gasp for breath. I force myself to breathe slowly. To breathe in and out. In and out.

My palms are wet. My mouth is dry. I'm shaking all over. I try to focus on the sound of my dad snoring. Always annoying, now comforting.

But there is something out there. *For real!* I can hear it. It's banging on the bear locker. Claws raking across metal. The earth beneath our tent reverberates with the thump of padded paws.

This is no dream! Not this time! But as in the dream I had of flying, the chill I feel verges on thrill. I poke my head out of the tent to see if what I hear is a grizzly.

From our tent all I can see is a huge bulk of darkness. A living shadow. Nosing up to the bear locker, less than ten feet away.

I think again of the Boy Scout who, according to Ranger Pam, "lost his life." I've heard about grizzlies pulling people out of their tents and eating them.

I've *dreamt* about it, too! *Just moments ago!*

I pull my head back into my tent.

But what good is a tent going to be against a grizzly?

I poke my head back out at what I'm now *positive* is a grizzly bear. I swear I can see the hump on its back. I can smell it. Damp fur, rank breath.

Death.

Is it moving toward the tent now? In the darkness I can't tell.

The confining space of the tent tightens around me. I can't breathe. Should I wake my dad?

The grizzly snorts once, scrapes the ground with huge claws, and snorts again.

It's time to wake my dad!

DAY FOUR

A GRAVEYARD
OF BOATS

D ad! Dad! There's a grizzly outside!"

Immediately, Dad snaps to attention, sitting up like a jack-in-the-box. He pokes his head out of the tent for a second, then grabs a can beside his sleeping bag and starts shaking it—*hard!* It sounds like there are coins in the can. It's like a metallic rattle.

I start clapping my hands together and yelling, "Go away, Bear! There's no food in here!"

Unless, of course, it decides *we're* food.

The grizzly swings its massive head toward us, chuffs—steam blowing out of its huge nostrils—then swings away, slowly, and slowly sways off into the greater darkness of the forest.

I stop yelling and clapping. And Dad stops shaking the can full of coins—which I hadn't seen before.

We look at each other.

And *breathe.*

Dad puts down the can. Then he puts a hand on my

shoulder, and says, "Good job, Aaron. You kept your cool. I should've brought a whistle. Some people blow them to keep away bears. But they scare away all the other wildlife, too. But last night, I dropped some coins into this empty bean can before I went to sleep. Just in case."

Before I can say anything, he slides back down into his sleeping bag and says, "If you hear the bear again, shake the can. And wake me up."

I close the tent flap and try to sleep, but I'm too excited. Nothing like a grizzly to give you that jolt of caffeine!

Wish I had my iPod. Music would help me calm down. I miss my music.

I try to slow my breathing, and after awhile, for the first time, I hear the distant roar of the Chute. It's been there all along, but I didn't notice it above the sounds of the forest. A deep, rushing roar, muffled by trees. Like the wind through the forest. A dark wind.

* * *

In the morning we inspect the grizzly's tracks. They circle the bear locker, come near our tent, then lead back up toward the mountains.

I'm glad I cached the food. I'm in no mood to go hungry for the rest of the trip. And I'm in no mood to be a meal *for* a grizzly, drawn to our tent because of the smell of food.

I tell Dad about my dreams: the beast, the grizzly

chasing me, and then the grizzly crashing into our tent. It seemed so real.

"Some dreams become real," he says. "They become who you are. They reflect your fears, your wishes."

While Dad starts a fire, I write the grizzly dreams in my journal. No way are they about my wishes, that's for sure! Then I write about the real grizzly and the tracks it left behind.

We eat breakfast and break camp, speaking only when necessary, the grizzly always in the back of my mind. Now we stow our gear in the cargo holds and get ready for the Chute. I tell Dad that I want to sit in the aft cockpit again, in back. I want to control the kayak through the rapids.

"Not a good idea, Aaron. Your shoulder's hurt and with the high, fast, snowmelt water this could be dangerous."

"My shoulder's fine!" That's a lie. It's still crazy sore, but I've been banged up worse from spills at local skate parks.

"We've got to be able to turn on a dime," Dad says. "I really don't think this is the right time for you."

"*Survival,* Dad. Self-confidence. Remember? That's what you've been harping about. How am I supposed to build up my self-confidence if you never give me a chance? Last night you said, 'Good job!' Now we're back to you always being boss. You just don't trust me. I can do this!"

"There's too much at risk here, Aaron. If we wreck the kayak on the rocks. . . . We don't know when the next boat's coming along. And we could lose all our gear and food. I don't know, Aaron. Maybe on the Cariboo River. That's supposed to be a real challenge too, but maybe not quite as dangerous as this."

"I'm sitting in the back! If you don't trust me with this you can hike around the Chute and meet me at the other end. I'll run it myself!"

Dad takes a deep breath, then is quiet for a moment. "Okay, okay," he says after awhile. "You win! You did keep your cool last night. You didn't panic. Now this is against my better judgment, but—"

"Thanks for the vote of confidence, *Dad!*" But I smile a bit when I say it, because he gave in, after all.

We climb into the kayak—me in back—and push off. A family of harlequin ducks scatters among the reeds. The colorful papa duck makes a racket of quacks. I wonder if he's squawking at his son.

Now that we're out on the water I can hear the roar of the rapids loud and clear. The Chute starts right at the exit of Lake Isaac. I'm totally psyched! *Stoked!*

Normally the Chute's not supposed to be all that hard to run, but the moment we eddy out to take a look, I can see we're in for a wild ride. The volume from the spring snow-melt has pushed it up to the level of a real torrent, with treacherous obstacles still poking up above the water. Broken trees and huge boulders, like the slippery backs of hippos.

Remember, we're not in a river kayak, which you can turn on a dime. We're in a big, heavy lake kayak. I pull up the rudder so at least I can steer with my paddle.

Dad looks back at me, a most serious look on his face. Then he turns and faces forward.

We pull out of the eddy and back-paddle at the top of the Chute for a moment to check it out one more time.

Then I say, "Let's roll!" and we take off like a rocket, plunging through the first hole, and burst through a tall standing wave.

"Yee-*haw!*" I shout, like me and Cassidy did back in Desolation Canyon. "Bucking bronco!"

The current grips our kayak and I think Dad's yelling something at me, but I can't hear him over the roar of the rapids. I open my mouth to yell back but my mouth fills with water.

It's freezing! We're thrashing and bouncing down the rapids. Water explodes in our faces.

I've learned enough from sea kayaking to keep the nose pointed into the waves. I dig in and swerve us around a boulder. In the boulder's eddy on the down-river side, we see something that sends a chill through me deeper than any cold.

Half of a canoe.

It's wedged into the river bottom, the stern sloping up and out of the river.

I wonder where the other half is. And the people who were in it. I think about the Boy Scout who lost his life.

And now I remember what Dad had called the Chute:

A boat graveyard.

Are we next?

ROLLER COASTER

We swirl and weave down the Chute and enter a ninety-degree curve to the right that might be too tight for our long lake kayak. We get swept beneath some snags and sweepers—low overhanging tree branches—and when I dig in my paddle near the stern, so we can pivot to the right, the upper blade tangles in the branches.

Our kayak stops but the water keeps pushing and suddenly the boat swings sideways to the current.

We're going over!

At the last second I wrestle the paddle free from the overhanging branches and straighten the boat out. We duck beneath the limbs and break loose. The current takes us away.

But the bank is rushing up fast. A back eddy tries to pull the nose of our kayak around but we battle our way through it.

Now we see the bow of the busted canoe poking straight up between two boulders.

We're headed right for it.

Water gushes over it and up the sides of the boulders. The bow of the canoe trembles in the turmoil, but it's stuck there.

And we could get stuck too.

Twenty feet. Ten.

It rushes up at us like an angry gravestone, but I dig my paddle in, hard, and at the last second we slide around it.

Then we're at the inside elbow of the bend—waves pounding our hull and forcing it down, under water. We almost stall.

"Paddle, Dad!" I yell. *"Paddle harder!"*

He does what I ask. Maybe I'm the captain now.

And straining our arms, shoulders, backs, legs, we drive our blades through the churning waves . . .

. . . then burst out and rocket down the other side of the Chute.

A broken canoe paddle sticks out of a pile of rocks near the cut bank, like an amputated arm waving good-bye.

And then as quickly as we entered the Chute, we're all the way through it.

We glide for a moment in easy water and I'm about to let out a shout of victory, when we're snatched by the "Roller Coaster," as Dad called it.

I'd forgotten about the Roller Coaster!

Once again, the current grabs us and sweeps us away.

Immediately, I see how it got its name. It's fast and furious, with barf-inducing drops.

But also like a roller coaster, *it's fun!*

But we're not on rails and once again our fate is in our own hands, not some machine's.

And I'm in the back, guiding the two of us.

And we don't want our kayak to end up like the broken-in-half canoe.

The good news is that there are no more boulders and no more bends, just huge standing waves. So I drop the rudder in and we hold a straight course down the center of all the crazy turbulence . . .

. . . until, at last, we glide out into smooth water at the far end.

Can I breathe now?

* * *

We drift.

About a quarter mile later, Dad shouts and points. A warning sign.

I slow down and then back-paddle, trying to keep our kayak in place as I read the sign aloud: "Stop! Pull out! Cascades! Unpassable. Portage here!"

Cascades? Those are small *waterfalls!* Dad didn't say anything about waterfalls.

I can hear them, like a continuous boom of thunder, and see the mist rising above the first drop a few hundred yards down the Isaac River.

Now my dad does the craziest thing ever. He turns his

head and yells over his shoulder: "We're NOT pulling out, Aaron! We're gonna *run* it! We're gonna challenge our fate! CHALLENGE THE RIVER GODS!"

My heart drops, like it did plunging down the Roller Coaster. I can't believe my ears! I'm excited and furious and scared, all at the same time.

This is so unlike him! Cassidy might have wanted to shoot down cascades in a kayak—maybe even his dad, Wild Man Willie.

But not *Dad!*

"HERE WE GO, KIDDO!" he shouts. A grin spreads across my face.

And he starts paddling toward certain doom.

And I paddle with him.

DANGER!

Then just as suddenly, he stops paddling, turns back toward me, and shouts, "JUST *KIDDING!*"

Just kidding? *Whaaat? Kidding?* It's *not* funny!

Then again, maybe it is. . . .

I even grin, maybe clamping my teeth a little too hard.

Dad yells that we *have* to eddy out and portage around the cascades, and I'm not arguing. We find a large eddy and I angle our kayak into it and we slide into shore, a little disappointed. Just a little.

It's not until then that I look up and notice the scenery. The Cariboo Mountains are brilliant white, glittering in their veil of snow.

Dad steps out and pulls the nose of the kayak up onto shore, then grabs my arm as I climb out. Once I'm on land, he grabs my other arm and doesn't let go. His eyes sparkle as they stare into mine. "Gotcha, didn't I?" he says, a huge smile on his face. It's about as close to a hug as he's given me in a long, long time.

"Nah. I knew you were too chicken to run the cascades."

He laughs and I feel a rush of pride and almost hug him. But the kayak knocks against my knee and I break loose and scramble up the steep bank.

We have a hard portage ahead.

*　*　*

The shore is steep and muddy and the trail is by far the roughest portage we've taken yet. It's narrow and pocked with holes and studded with large rocks. We rig up the portage cart and Dad handles the bow and I push at the stern.

After awhile, we take a breather to look down at the thundering cascades below. I sit on a rock and fantasize about shooting it in a river kayak someday. I'd learn to roll it— something impossible to do in a fully-loaded, two-person lake kayak.

"Let's come back and run this in river kayaks someday. Okay, Dad?"

"I'd love that, Aaron." He gives me a lingering smile.

But the moment is broken when we start back down the trail. I take the lead, and maybe I'm thinking about the next trip instead of the present, and I let the right wheel roll over a big round stone and the cart flips over . . . *and starts sliding down toward the river!*

"*NOOOO!*" I shout as we sprint after it, slipping on our butts and sliding in the kayak's wake. We bounce down over roots and rocks, and watch as the rig crashes down toward the boiling cauldron of the cascades below.

Just when I think all is lost, the kayak snags on a gnarly root.

We slide down to it. Now all we have to do is haul it back up.

A half hour later, back up on the portage trail, everything's pretty well secured when Dad breaks his silence and snaps, "Aaron! You weren't paying attention! You've got to focus on what you're doing! This whole trip could've been ruined by your negligence!"

"Dad, it was an *accident!*"

I'm burning up with . . . what? Hurt pride? Anger? But I hold my tongue because, well, what's the use?

Sometimes I think that life with Dad is like shooting rapids, where success may be one stroke away from disaster. There are slow and easy parts—but then you always hit the rapids again.

* * *

After the portage we do another short paddle down Isaac River, and come to another big yellow sign:

DANGER!
Waterfall Ahead
Pull out canoes here

It's decorated with a drawing of a smashed canoe.

This portage starts out steep, but soon it's beautiful and lined with moss, and I don't have to worry about flipping the kayak and losing it again.

We take a short side trip to see the Isaac River Falls. It's small but still pretty awesome. A wall of white water crashes down thirty-six feet. We stand in the thundering mist for a bit, then get back to work.

The portage ends with a steep descent to McLeary Lake. A small, shallow gem of a lake set in the necklace of mountains.

"Why don't we camp here?" I say, and this time Dad agrees. It's been a short day, but a hard and hazardous one. And except for spilling the kayak, it's been a good day.

Dad even says, "Let's celebrate with the rest of the marshmallows after dinner!" When I tell him that I already ate them all he scratches his whiskers and gives me one of his looks.

Then he grins, and says, "I guess an extra ration of hot cocoa will have to do!"

No canned beans for dinner tonight. Dad breaks out a jar of marinara sauce and a box of spaghetti. I'm so hungry I could eat the box.

While the sauce simmers and we wait for the pasta water to boil, we sit on a log by the lake and watch a family of otters playing at the mouth of the river. They take turns slipping down a natural mud slide and—*WHOOSH!*—splashing

into the water, rolling down the current, then clambering out and trotting back up the slope, for another slide down.

As if inspired by the innocence of their game, Dad starts to talk about when he was a boy.

"It's funny, Aaron, but when I was your age, younger, I . . . well . . . I wanted to be a jazz musician. I wanted to go to New York City when I was old enough and play jazz piano in the clubs there. Can you believe that? New York City!" He shakes his head and stares down into his cup. The falls can still be heard in the distance. The breeze is scented with cedar and a hint of snow. I expect him to go on, but he stays silent.

It's almost dusk, the sunset clouds still like the afterglow of a forest fire on the peaks to the west. "The water's boiling," he says and gets up.

After dinner, Dad stirs the dying fire. Then he sighs and says, "My dad, your grandfather, he ridiculed me whenever I played jazz on the piano. He said nobody could make it as a jazz musician, especially not a white boy like me, since jazz and blues were invented by African Americans."

He pauses a moment, listening to the distant roar of the falls, and for the first time I notice the moon. It's over half full now, knocking a million stars clear out of the sky.

I look down into my mug of cocoa. The moon floats in the darkness, like the light at the end of a tunnel.

He sets his mug down on a rock and sticks a toothpick in his mouth. "I tried to tell him that the great jazz pianist Dave Brubeck was white. He was my hero. Him and Miles Davis, who was black. They were like two keys on a piano. One black, one white."

It's weird. Dad wanting to be a jazz musician. Me wanting to write rap songs. How ironic! He's always saying that hip-hop is black music, "urban" music, and that it's not my culture. He says: *Forget rap. Hit the books and learn a skill.* One time I asked him, "What about Macklemore? And Eminem? They're white."

Dad said, "They're one in a million! Or two."

So maybe I'm one in a million too. "Well, what about me?" I say now, resting my cup on my thigh. "It's the same thing. I'm white and I want to write hip-hop songs. You're white and you wanted to be a jazz musician!"

Dad almost laughs. Then he shakes his head again and looks down. "It's not the same, Aaron, though I see your point. I took piano lessons starting at age five. My piano instructor told me I had talent. You have talent too, but it's not writing rap songs. It's writing poetry and stories. I read a poem you wrote in seventh grade that knocked my socks off. You have a gift for language, Aaron. You just have to learn to develop your craft."

I'm flattered. He likes my writing! But something in me rises up. "Aren't you being a hypocrite? You're just trying to control me, the way your dad did you!"

This time he does laugh, though it sounds almost like a sob. "I think you've got me there. But I'm not trying to control you so much as guide you, Aaron. That's what dads are for, I guess."

It still sounds like hypocrisy to me, but I don't say it. I don't know what to say.

Then Dad says, "Time to hit the hay, Aaron. Tomorrow's another big day." He smiles, then gets up and goes to the tent. I sit for a while and watch the flames dancing like ghosts in the fire.

The last thing I hear, when I finally snuggle down into my sleeping bag—over the sound of the falls, over the sound of everything—is Dad's snoring. I push his elbow and he rolls over and is quiet.

* * *

In the morning I wake to the sound of something huge crashing through the underbrush. Right toward our tent.

What now?

RACING BACKWARDS

On all fours I peek out of the opening to our tent. A massive bull moose gallops past us, close enough that I feel a breeze in my hair, and charges straight into McLeary Lake with a great splash.

He snorts his way across the marshy shallows, thrashing his knees. In a matter of minutes, he swims across the deeper middle, chugging like a steam engine, and at the far end he scrambles out, dripping duckweed and moose snot, and rubs his giant rack against a willow. Then charges off into the bush.

All that's left of the bizarre encounter is the distant roar of the falls.

What could there be out there to scare a huge bull moose like that?

A wolf pack? A grizzly?

I look up at the enormous Cariboo Glacier, glowing in the early morning sunshine. A bald eagle pierces the silence and settles on the upper branches of a tall tree. Just below it, four more bald eagles crouch, watching down at me with hooded eyes.

* * *

We're out on the lake by 9 A.M. No clouds, but we're in the shadow of the mountains, so it will be awhile till the sun tops the ridge to bless us.

McLeary Lake is small. We paddle in silence, and in no time we're at the point where the lake flows into the Cariboo River, fed by the great Cariboo Glacier.

Dad breaks a long silence with the warning: "Careful now, Aaron. I read that the Cariboo River can be the most challenging part of the trip."

What? Harder than the Chute? No way.

I'm in the stern, so it's my job to control the way we maneuver through whatever's coming. I'm up to it. And suddenly all my senses sharpen to a point as the river picks up speed. It's as if I just woke up from a long sleep.

We're flowing fast between towering mountain peaks. Snowfields and cascading waterfalls glisten above us. The Cariboo River is glacial meltwater, aqua blue, with lots of silt in it and an insanely powerful current.

And it's getting even faster. And the faster the current the faster we have to paddle. As I learned in river rafting, you have to stay faster than the current. You have to control the direction the kayak takes or the current will control it for you.

After about a mile we come around a bend into a maze of snags and sweepers. I must find the right channel.

NOW!

The current's forcing us toward the inside curve of the river, and we must fight to get away from the shore. If we hit bottom, we'll tumble like a log in a flood.

Sure enough, the bottom of our kayak scrapes across a submerged tree and almost tips us in the shallows. We instinctively dig our blades into the silt, our paddles almost vertical. But we're snagged on the tree and the current is pushing us over.

I need to lighten the load, so I leave my paddle in my cockpit and swing my legs over the side, one by one— the spray skirt still around my waist—and step into the thigh-high water. The kayak rises off the submerged log and almost pulls free from my grasp. If Dad jumps out too, and we lose our grip, we could lose our kayak. I've got to try to push us out into the main current and jump back in before the kayak capsizes—or runs wild, without me in it. Stooped over, bracing my feet against the tricky bottom, I push the stern with all my might, and yell, "Dad! *Paddle!*"

Dad paddles furiously, which makes it even more challenging for me to jump back into the kayak without tipping it over. But if I can't get back in Dad'll be heading solo down the river, paddling in the front with no real control. He'll flip for sure.

Just before the boat takes off without me, I fling myself

over the hull just behind my seat and try to pull myself into the cockpit on my belly. I grab my paddle with one hand while holding on to the rim of my cockpit with the other, and jab my paddle blade into the river bottom to push us away from shore.

At one point I'm headfirst *inside* the cockpit, my head where my feet should be! The cockpit's filling with water and I'm drowning in it! I'm gagging and spluttering and kicking wildly, trying to back out and sit up at the same time.

If you saw this on YouTube you'd laugh like crazy, but I'm not laughing.

As soon as I get myself turned around and seated, we're pushed into a sweeper and a branch almost takes my head off. But I slip my paddle into the leg space and use both my hands to pull us back along the branch until an eddy grabs the tail of the kayak and spins us free.

But the rudder's up and I haven't yet retrieved my

paddle, and before I know it *we're racing backwards down the river, tail first!* Like riding a roller coaster backwards. I try to drop the rudder in and grab my paddle at the same time, but the tail is swinging wildly, dangerously, and before I can release the rudder I can feel our kayak rolling over. I know it.

We're going to capsize!

THE END OF OUR TRIP AS WE KNOW IT

We're capsizing and Dad's yelling and I'm trying to get my paddle out and use it to pivot us around.

In a blind act of desperation I do just that. I decide to leave the rudder up and grab my paddle and dig it in. The kayak spins just enough for Dad to back-paddle and swing us counterclockwise until we're nose first again—just in time to swerve past a logjam . . .

. . . and into smoother, slower water.

Whew!

Dad says something over his shoulder, but I am too busy letting out a whoop of joy. I'm still trembling, but we're safe now, and I know what I did was awesome. I wouldn't mind hearing it from my dad, though.

Then Dad says something over his shoulder again. It sounds like, "Well done!" But that can't be right.

"What?"

"That was amazing, Aaron. You did well!"

Yes!

We glide for a couple of miles, barely paddling, until the Cariboo empties into Lanezi Lake. Even then, we're still wet and shaken. But speaking just for myself: It was *fun!* A scary kind of fun. A total adrenaline rush, fighting-for-your-life type of fun.

And now we're floating on this knockout gorgeous lake, with the mountains rising almost right up out of the water. Birds and mountains are reflected in the lake and I feel like we're flying through the sky.

All of a sudden I'm hungry. I'm *starving!* "Dad!" I say. "Let's pull over and eat!"

Dad keeps paddling, like he doesn't even hear me. *"Dad!"*

"I'm thinking!" he says, without easing his stroke.

We slide by creeks shooting into the lake, white with glacial meltwater, and past skinny waterfalls crashing straight down, losing themselves in plumes of mist.

I have no choice but to get back into the rhythm of paddling. Geez, we survived some comical mishaps that could've turned tragic at any moment, and Dad says, "Well done!" But then nothing.

Not a word.

I guess I just can't get enough praise.

And once again I get lost in the maze of my thoughts.

* * *

We paddle two-thirds the length of the long lake, my stomach gnawing on itself, and then Dad almost floors me.

"Okay, Aaron. How 'bout we call it a day and do some fishin'?"

"Sweet! Awesome! Let's *do* it!" We haven't fished once on the whole trip. There's been no time. We've been eating freeze-dried or out of cans, and struggling with the elements, and just trying to stay alive.

Dad points toward a campsite on a flat of land next to a small, rushing creek. The sun's still high. There's not a cloud in the sky.

First we eat some pepperoni sticks, and peanut butter on dry buns, as we set up camp. Dad says the sun's too hot yet for fishing, we should wait till it dips behind the peaks. I lean against a boulder near the water, open my spiral-bound notebook, and work on my journal.

This morning, a massive bull moose galloped past us. . . .

I write so fast that my handwriting looks like Arabic. A lot's happened since yesterday. I'm surprised by how much I want to write. How good it feels to put it all on the page.

The sun's like a warm hand on my back. The water is still. A few birds twitter. And for the first time on this trip I realize I don't miss hip-hop. I don't miss my cell phone or my iPod or even my skateboard. And I don't feel angry, or frustrated, or trapped. I feel strong and peaceful. When I see a beaver gliding by, maybe fifty yards out, I raise two fingers and shout, "Peace out!"

I know this peace can't last, but I try to enjoy it while it does.

After an hour or two of writing, I feel a shadow slide over me. The sun's sunk behind an imposing peak. I think it's Ishpa Mountain. I'll have to look at the map.

I shut my notebook and set it down beside me. There's an almost physical sense of satisfaction after writing well for a long period of time. It's like flexing new muscles. It feels a little like a good paddle through rough water, followed by a smooth stretch of river.

Dad's fiddling with his fishing gear in front of the tent. "Hey, Dad, can you hook me up with a fishing rod?" I chuckle at my unintended pun, but it flies right over Dad's head.

"Look at this," he says. He points at a large, overturned rock. Then he points at a set of deep claw marks about ten feet up the trunk of a nearby tree. "Bear sign," he says.

"Awesome!" I want to see a bear again, especially a grizzly. I just don't want to see it like right in my face, or right behind me, coming for me.

Dad gives me a look. Then he says, "Here." He hands me a rod still broken down into three parts. "You can rig it, right? Or do you want me to do it for you?"

"I'm good." I take the rod and he hands over his tackle box. I go back and lean against my boulder. Okay, I think. I can do this.

It takes some fumbling but I get my rod all rigged out, with a shiny spoon lure that has a medium-sized hook.

We cross the powerful little creek, stepping carefully on

mossy stones, and look for a good place to fish. I've got my rod in one hand and a fishing net in the other. Dad's carrying his rod and the orange plastic tackle box.

We cast our lines just past the riffle at the mouth of a larger creek, among the reeds in the blue-green lake, and reel in slowly, trying not to get snagged. We spread farther apart when our lines almost cross.

The snowy peaks above us, the tall cedars, the quiet mountain lake—it's all right out of *National Geographic*.

I won't mention the giant deerflies flying off with giant chunks of our flesh.

"Dad," I say, flicking away a fly.

"Mmm?" He's in quiet mode, or fishing mode, not speaking.

"Uhh, well, I've been wondering," I say anyway. "Remember how I'm supposed to write, like, a story based on this trip, right? For some reason a name for it came to me like, *BOOM!* when Ms. Dunn gave me my assignment. GRIZZLY PEAK. Crazy! But a good title, right? Anyway, I've been wondering if there is a mountain called Grizzly Peak around here anywhere. I mean with all the grizzlies that live in these mountains, you'd think one would be called Grizzly Peak. Anyway, if there is—or if there's one on the way home and we have time—well, I'd really like to see if we could climb it! I mean, all the way to the top. How awesome would *that* be? It would be like the perfect ending to my story, right? And—"

Dad interrupts me. "We'll see, Aaron. We'll see." Like he's not really listening. "Now it's time to catch a fish, and you've got to be quiet to catch a fish."

Right. Quiet. But I don't say it. I wouldn't want to scare away some fish that's listening in, now would I?

* * *

Time ticks by but nobody's counting the seconds. We toss out our lines, slap our arms, and reel in slowly. A couple of fish strike our lures but glance off. Maybe our hooks are too big.

Finally, I get a strike and it holds. "Got something, Dad!" There's a sharp tug, a white splash, and a living rainbow flashes and dances two feet above the surface! My rod bends and bounces in my hands. I loosen the drag, and let the fighting fish play itself out.

When it stops tiptoeing across the water, I start reeling quickly, wading in up to my shins.

And when I can see the sheen of color breaking the surface, I reach in and scoop it up with my net.

"Dad! A rainbow trout!" I do a little dance.

"Dinner!" Dad grins.

The trout, still flapping and flopping, is about a foot long.

"Yeah," I say. "Dinner for *me!* You catch your own!"

After about an hour Dad finally catches two, about ten inches apiece. He lets me carry the stringer of trout back to our camp. And he "lets" me clean them too. But I don't mind because this evening we eat a mess of rainbows grilled over an open fire, and it's the best meal I've had since the fresh-caught salmon off Bella Bella.

Okay, the skin's a little burnt. Black, actually. But the flesh is tender and juicy. It flakes off like rose petals and melts in your mouth.

We eat and talk about fishing, and Dad for the first time says, "I wish your mother was here. And Sean too."

We lick our fingers and act as if nothing bad has happened between us over the last few months, before and after my getting kicked out of school.

The twilight is so soft, the hour still so early, we decide to take "a little spin"—as Dad calls it—out on the lake, and watch the stars come out one by one. We paddle, we float, then paddle some more. When we notice the moon making its appearance, growing plump and content in the sky, we head back.

As we pull into camp, we see a huge shadow hunched over the dying coals of our fire.

And it's the end of our trip as we know it!

MOON BEAR

Chaos.

There's a grizzly bear devouring our food! Based on its enormous size, I'd guess it's a male. Without thinking—as with the bull moose—I paddle *toward* the grizzly, Dad paddles away. But about ten feet offshore, I stop paddling and we both start yelling and slashing our paddles, hoping to scare the grizzly away.

"*GO AWAY, BEAR!*" I yell.

"*SCRAM!*" shouts Dad. "*SHOO!*"

The grizzly slowly stands up to check us out, and in the moonlight we can make out an unusual white patch, round like a full moon, on his hairy chest. He chuffs and a puff of steam floats from his mouth.

Then he drops back down to all fours, lowers his great head, and with a loud roar charges into the lake. *Right at us.* Crashing across the shallows.

We're back-paddling like crazy, yelling, pure panic, but I'm in the back and I've got to steer.

I plunge my paddle vertically and pivot us around so we can forward paddle. I don't have to tell Dad. We start paddling for our lives and we don't look back.

But I can hear the grizzly huffing and splashing behind us, maybe five feet away.

Then, just as suddenly, I don't hear him.

We coast in a big loop in the growing moonlight and look back. Griz is on his way back toward our camp.

We float there a moment, catching our breath, not saying anything.

Then Dad says, "We better head back—not too close

—and hope we can scare him off. We left our food out. . . ."
He trails off.

We paddle back and watch the big bear bumble out of the lake and up the low bank—and sure enough, he heads right for our food. He snatches up our biggest wet bag in his massive jaws and lazily ambles away.

"Our food!" I yell. What's left of it, anyway.

But the grizzly crashes through the brush and is gone.

We almost tip the kayak in our rush to get ashore. We splash through the shallows and race up the low bank. The grill's been toppled over, the fire scattered. Embers pulse with fire glow, charred wood still smokes, coal-blackened stones have been knocked five feet from the ring.

Not a scrap of food is left behind.

Dad swears but he's not swearing at me. He blames himself for wanting to "take a spin" in the kayak before securing the camp from bears.

He checks to see that the tent's okay, and our clothes bags. Then finds my daypack near the boulder where I left it. He picks it up. It dangles from his fingers in shreds. All that's left of the gorp is gone. Even my secret stash of candy is gone. Snickers bars, English toffee. The plastic container of peanut butter is missing.

On the ground, splattered with wrapper shreds and bits of chocolate, is my notebook. The spiral wiring looks a little bent out of shape, but otherwise the notebook is all in one piece.

But that doesn't stop Dad from lighting into me. "Aaron! I *told* you never to leave your notebook lying around. Without your journal you can't complete your assignment and graduate!"

I can't believe my ears. He's mad about my notebook, not our food being gone!

"Chill, Dad! *Geez!* You're the one who screwed up, not me!"

"We both messed up! I'm sorry, I'm losing it here. But the food at this point is less important than your notebook. We can catch fish, but—"

"But nothing! I have a good memory! I don't *need* the notebook to write my story. But now we have **no food left!**" I yell. "No pepperoni sticks. No peanut butter. No cooking oil. No salt. No hot chocolate. No pasta. No bread. No cheese. No sugar for our coffee. In fact—*no coffee!*"

"Get a grip!" Dad says.

"Oh no! My assignment!" I yell, picking up my dusty notebook and waving it around. "I will fail if I lose my journal. I won't graduate middle school. I won't go to high school. I won't go to college. I may as well—" I start choking on my own sarcasm.

And then I start to cry. It's like when a campfire collapses in upon itself. Sparks fly and smoke rises, then the fire falls to its knees, hissing and spluttering.

I don't know how it happens, or why, but suddenly I'm on my knees in Dad's arms. He's cradling me. He's rocking me. He's shushing me. But tears are streaming down *his* cheeks, not mine. I'm teary-eyed, yes, but I'm quiet. And all I know is that it's getting harder and harder to always be so angry at him. He's wrong half the time—maybe more than half the time—but he's my dad.

Sometimes it's a battle. But he cares about me. I know that.

And sometimes, like me—well, less often than me—he just loses it. His cool. His temper.

* * *

Later, in the tent, while Dad sleeps, I think about the Moon Bear, as I've come to call him. I've never heard of a grizzly bear with a white moon on its chest, but there's a whole lot I don't know about yet, I guess.

As I drift off to sleep, I wonder if the grizzly that chased me in the skateboard dream was a premonition of the Moon Bear. And what about the grizzly I dreamed about smashing into our tent?

"Some dreams become real." That's what Dad said.

* * *

In the first light of dawn, I shake myself from a series of dreams. I can still see them, sharp and clear. Dreams about the Moon Bear climbing a mountain. Like scenes from a movie.

I open the flap a bit to let in the light, pick up my pen, and write in my journal:

In the dreams the Moon Bear sometimes whimpers and sometimes roars. He's sometimes scary and sometimes not. But he always carries the moon up the mountain. Sometimes he holds it at his chest. Sometimes he carries it over his head or on his shoulders. Sometimes he pushes it like a boulder. But he always moves up and up. And when he almost reaches the top, he always slips and falls, tumbling back down, and the moon comes tumbling after him. And then at the bottom, he gets up, lifts the moon, and starts up again. No matter how high he climbs, the mountain always rises above him.

FISH BUT NO FIRE

I drop my pen, close the flap, and finally drift back to sleep.

We wake to the crack of thunder. Lightning illuminates the inside of our tent, followed by more claps of thunder and flashes of lightning.

Then the rain comes pounding down like nails. The tent ripples and sags and whips in the wind.

It's well into morning but we're not going anywhere. I think about last night. The crying. And my dreams about the grizzly. The Moon Bear.

"Dad," I say, "I'm hungry. And I want coffee." I feel like a little kid.

"We'll go fishing when this blows over." Dad uncorks a loud one and the tent fills with killer gas.

"Are you kidding me? *Seriously!*" I open the tent flap and try to wave the fumes away. I get a cold face full of rain and shut the flap before we're soaked.

"We're lucky," Dad says.

"Why? Because we haven't been hit by lightning?

That could happen any moment now." I slide back into my sleeping bag.

"We're lucky the bear didn't destroy our tent. I snapped at you last night about your notebook—but what I was really shook up about was the grizzly. There was a short film at the ranger station about grizzlies. It showed one ripping a tent to shreds while a camper was still inside."

I wonder what happened to that camper. I feel a chill running through me, and it's not from the cold.

"That's why you don't keep food in your tent," he says.

"*We're* food." I pull my bag up around my head.

"Could be," he says. "When I was Googling Bowron Lakes I read a blog about a horrific bear mauling. It was at a camp on one of these lakes. One camper died and the other was pinned inside a cabin while the grizzly kept trying different ways to break in. It's rare but it does happen."

"Geez, Dad! If you're trying to scare me you're doing a pretty good job." I can't shake the image of a grizzly trying to bite and claw his way inside the cabin.

Or our tent. It's like that dream I had about a grizzly pushing his great head into our tent. And then I think of my last journal entry this morning, the dream about the grizzly carrying the moon up the mountain.

The more I think about it the more I'm sure that both grizzlies are the same bear.

I want to tell Dad about it, or, better yet, show him what I wrote. But before I can get a word out, he says, "Actually,

Aaron, we went about it all wrong. According to the film you're not supposed to shout or move quickly when encountering a grizzly. You're supposed to talk softly, calmly, slowly back away, and keep facing them while avoiding direct eye contact. A grizzly can outrun a man. Hell, they're as fast as a race horse. And climbing a tree won't do you any good— they can chase you right up!"

"Well, whatever we did, it worked." I grin. "It did run off. Eventually."

"Like I said, we're lucky." He grins back.

"Well, I'm still hungry," I groan. "And I still want my coffee." It's so cold in our tent, little puffs of cloud come out every time we talk.

"This is the bare bones of survival, Aaron," he says, suddenly very serious. "With luck, we'll be out of here in two days, counting today. From now on we have to fish for our food and do without coffee and sugar and beef jerky. But really, it'll be good for us. We can do this."

I know we can, but I don't say it out loud. I'm not sure how "good" it'll be for us, but something stirs in me. Surviving in the wild. Out in the elements. It's intense. Suddenly I don't feel like a little boy anymore. I feel like a young adult. A man, even.

Well, almost.

And just as suddenly the rain stops and the sun pierces the gloom. The tree branches drip and the lake laps against the shore.

* * *

We fish for breakfast. But fishing for breakfast on an empty stomach is a real challenge. Have you ever gone to school on an empty stomach? Spent the whole morning on an empty stomach? Not fun.

We go to the same spot we went to yesterday, but the only things biting are the mosquitoes and deerflies.

After an hour we've only caught one fish between us. I hooked it and Dad scooped it up with the net. A small trout, not more than eight inches long. Maybe two or three bites each.

Maybe we'll have to eat the eyeballs.

We keep fishing, but nothing happens. No fish jump. Silence. They must be hiding in the shallows, biding their time.

My stomach grumbles. It growls. I could eat a bear.

But it's not until we get back to camp, a couple of hours later and still with just the one small trout dangling from the stringer, that we start to get a real sense of what hunger means.

We look for our last box of wooden matches. Where could it be?

There it is: in the mud near the fire ring. In the chaos of the Moon Bear's raid, they'd been left out all night! And in the rain this morning.

We groan. I pick up the matchbox and the cardboard falls apart in my hands. I look inside. Matches float in a puddle, like tiny kayaks in a tiny lake. Then they spill out in a tiny waterfall down onto the muddy ground.

We have fish, but we don't have fire!

Great, I think. Just great.

Dad swears, then picks the matches out of the mud, one by one, and sets them on a stone to try to dry them in the sun.

Only the sun is hiding behind a cloud.

"Don't you have, like, a lighter, Dad?"

"I don't smoke, Aaron. Remember?" He looks at me like I'm a nut. I look back at him like he's a nut. We stand there.

We don't know what to do.

All I know is we may have to eat sashimi from now on— raw fish, without rice or soy sauce. Or chopsticks.

"I'll look for something to burn," I say, and head off to look for some dry wood, just in case we get a match to flare.

I find a few moss- and lichen-covered scraps under a rock overhang and bundle them into my arms. Not exactly dry.

When I get back, I see Dad trying to strike the matches against stone. Most just snap in two. But a couple spark and go out, thin wisps of smoke disappearing into air. They're still pretty soaked, and I'm not sure they'll ever totally dry out.

"Man!" I say, holding my small load of kindling. "Let me try."

"Go for it," he says, and stands up, pressing his hands against the base of his back.

Then I squat down and place the lichen-covered kindling above some twigs Dad had set atop the wet ashes in the fire ring, and I stick a twist of newspaper he had prepared beneath the wood.

I strike a match against stone. It sparks and snaps in two and goes out. I strike another one, a little gentler, and the head drops off.

I concentrate. I focus. I take a deep breath—and on my third match the head bursts into flame! I cup my hand and ease the lighted match down to the twist of newspaper, slowly, slowly.

The paper flares up and I lean down and gently blow on it, coaxing it, until the flames crawl across the kindling and—*PRESTO!*—we have a small fire going!

"Good job, Aaron!"

But I look again and see that the wood is smoking, the flame is dwindling. Still too much moisture in it, I guess.

And then I see that the rows of matches laid out on the stump have dwindled. *There are only eight matches left!* For tonight and all day tomorrow. They have become as precious as gold. And who knows how many of them will light?

If any.

While Dad guts and cleans our one small trout, I gather more stray scraps of wood and try to coax the fire, hoping for a little luck. When Dad's done, he lays the slim slab of fish on the not-quite-hot grill.

We have a spatula but no oil, no salt, no pepper, no lemon, nothing. Nothing but appetites as big as a bear's.

In a couple of minutes, Dad lifts the fish from the grill with his spatula to flip it over—but it slides off and lands in the dirt! Dad swears.

Then we see that the fire is sputtering out.

Dad snatches the gutted trout off the ground with his fingers, tips his water bottle over it to clean the dirt off, then flops it back on the grill.

Which is now barely warm.

I haven't said anything. If I had dropped the fish, I hate to think what Dad would have said.

I look at the last of the matches, but with the wood around here still so damp, I think maybe it would be better to try them later. *If* the rain doesn't come back, and *if* the wood eventually dries.

As if hearing my thoughts, Dad says, "Want some sushi? Actually, it might be almost half cooked."

"Or half raw," I say. And we both try to grin. Sad little grins.

With his spatula he lifts the half-raw trout off the luke-warm grill, and slices it in two.

Yep. Inside, the fish looks almost raw. Dad pokes it, then serves me the half with the head still attached.

I look down at it for a long moment. Then I say to the fish head, "Thanks, dude!" It's my kind of grace.

I pick it up with my fingers and eat all the meat I can get to—three yucky bites. A little like slimy gum—but not sweet.

In fact it's probably the worst thing I ever ate.

I force myself to swallow, as I stare down at the fish eye-balls staring back up at me.

The half-raw fish is gone, but I'm still super hungry. My stomach is growling louder than ever.

THE MONSTER'S COILS

Dad grabs the fish head when I finish with it. He plucks out an eyeball, pops it in his mouth, and chews it slowly, licking his lips. "Best part, kiddo. *Um-hmmm*. And good for ya too!"

Gross! I think. But if he can do it so can I.

I pluck out the other eyeball and pop it into my mouth like a grape.

PFOOW! I spit it out and watch it roll across the ground.

"*Gross!*" I yell it this time. "That tasted like . . . like an *eyeball!*"

I'd rather go hungry.

I try to rinse out the taste with water while Dad licks each finger, like he was eating a buffalo wing or something. Then we break camp on empty stomachs.

* * *

Lanezi Lake funnels back into the Cariboo River. We're running on empty, but we're not letting that slow us down.

We're lean mean paddling machines. The quicker we can get to our next campsite, probably on Unna Lake, the sooner we can fish again.

Ducks scatter out of our way. Snowy mountains slide by. The sky is clear blue here, scudded with clouds there, ever changing.

We're racing against our bellies.

My mind's no longer like a maze. It's focused. It's like an arrow flying toward >>>> *FOOD*.

We're moving so fast that we almost miss the channel into Sandy Lake. I'm in back. I execute a left pivot in the nick of time. The lake's shallow with sandspits sticking way out into the lake. Around us, the cedars have turned to pine, the mountains to snow-dusted hills.

We only pause to drink water from our bottles. There's a cool breeze but the sun is hot. Sweat stings our eyes. We need salt.

And we need food. I'd give anything for a bag of chips!

We keep paddling.

After Sandy Lake we fly down another river passage and then turn into the narrow entrance to Unna Lake. A tiny, enchanted gem, crystal clear. Awesome. Down below our kayak, we can see schools of small fish—too small to catch—darting in zigs and zags, as if with one intention:

Get away.

Although it's still early afternoon, we find a good spot beneath some aspen trees, and set up camp on high speed.

The plan is to fish now, *eat,* and then maybe take a hike up to nearby Cariboo Falls, if we have the energy.

Easier said than done. It's too sunny for good fishing. The fish are sleeping, hanging low along the bottom, or in the reeds.

But we fish, anyway. No choice. We're hungry.

We fish the reeds and snag our lures and catch nothing but duckweed. I lose one lure and Dad loses two. After two hours we're about to give up when Dad pulls in a little lake trout. It will have to do.

But we use up half the remaining matches to get a fire going.

That leaves *four!*

I try not to think about the future. I'm living in the now. At least this time the fire burns long enough to cook the fish.

Again I eat my share of fish in four or five bites, but this time I chew slowly, savoring the taste, trying to make it last.

And no, I don't eat the eyeballs.

There are no mosquitoes in the warm sun. Even the deerflies seem to be sleeping. Dad says he feels like a nap, but I remind him that we were going to go to Cariboo Falls. And now that we've eaten, I feel like we could make it.

"We'll go in the morning," he says. He yawns, lies back on the ground, and cradles his head in his crossed arms.

"Tomorrow we won't have the *energy* to hike up to the falls. We'll probably be starving. Come on, Dad. Let's go! It'll be cool!"

"You go, I'll nap." He pops a toothpick into his mouth and smiles.

"Geez, Dad! You told me they're like five times the size of the Isaac River Falls. Epic!" I can't believe myself. I'm actually begging my dad to come with me. A day ago I would've been deliriously happy to just go by myself.

What happened? Something has changed.

"Come on, Dad, you promised! We have to see the falls!" I punch his shoulder. *I actually punch his shoulder!* If he'd done that to me a few days ago I would've slugged him. *Hard!*

"Okay, okay!" Dad sits up. "First just let me rinse off!" He pulls off his grimy flannel shirt, kneels by the lake, and splashes water into his face and under his arms. I can see he's lost weight on this trip, and he was already skinny.

At this rate he'll be all skin and bones. And a scraggly beard.

But right now I'm practically running in place, raring to go. I'm totally psyched about climbing the falls. It's sort of like a sugar high, but I'm suddenly aware it's really a *hunger* high. I read something about it one time, maybe in a story by Ernest Hemingway. I can't remember. Whatever. I'm bursting with hungry energy, my mind as sharp as an ice pick.

"We'll climb the falls," I say. "Then we'll come back and fish when the sun is down and the fish are jumping."

Isn't that like the song? *Summertime . . . and the fish are . . . de duh duh . . .* Something like that. One of Dad's old bluesy jazz tunes.

Dad slaps his face three more times, climbs to his feet, and slips back into his flannel shirt, only buttoning it half-way up. His chest hair is like a thick rug.

I start off before he can catch up. It's an easy walk uphill, less than a mile. Through the cedar trees we can hear the roar of the falls in the distance. As the trail starts to dip the roar grows louder and louder.

I'm not prepared for what comes next. Instead of climbing the waterfall, we come to a drop-off, just above Cariboo Falls, and look down.

"*Awesome!*" I say. So much POWER! The thundering falls blast through a narrow canyon, rush over a ledge, and plunge down, sending up a powerful back spray that rises into the sky, creating a hazy, glowing rainbow in the sunlight.

Dad comes to my side. We just stand there, in a kind of awe. The falls are so fast and wide and powerful. And at the bottom the water churns and gallops like a herd of wild white horses.

I wipe the mist from my face and say, "Let's climb down!"

"I don't know, Aaron. Looks dangerous."

"Oh my god! *Dad!* Come on! It's a *challenge,* right?"

"That it is," he says. "But it's not for me. You go, if you really want to. But be careful! I'll watch." He bites his lip, looking worried. But then his grin splits his dark whiskers.

This time I don't argue. I'm too psyched. I take one more look down the falls and say, "Okay. Here goes!"

I scramble down like a mountain goat, leaping from one mossy, mist-soaked rock to the next.

Suddenly, my feet fly out from under me.

"WHOA!" I scream.

I'm falling. I'm going to plunge into the boiling cauldron below. I flail my arms and legs and crash on my side about ten feet below where I last jumped. I tumble head over heels, and slide down until I finally grab hold of a root and stop my fall. The root is clinging to a narrow rock ledge, which I pull myself up onto. It looks like I've fallen about halfway down from the top—maybe sixty feet. Maybe more.

Nice move, Aaron.

The wind is knocked out of me, my left side hurts like

hell, and I'm being hammered by the full force of the water-fall. The ledge slopes and it's slippery, so I cling to the root.

"*Aaron!*" Dad calls. I can barely hear him above the roar.

"*Hang on! I'm coming!*" Dad's coming. All I have to do is hang on.

But I can't!

The water's pounding down on me. I'm losing my grip. The blast of the waterfall is like a hurricane at my back.

Next thing I know, I'm dangling below the ledge, spinning. I've still got a hold of the root, thank God. But either my arm is going to tear from my body or it's going to tear from the thin root.

Dad is coming. I can tell because little rocks are bouncing down over my head.

But I can't hold on any longer.

I'm slipping, slipping. . . .

Suddenly Dad is there, reaching out to me. . . .

Too late! The root slides out of my hand.

Dad's hands grip my arm like a vice, but it's too late. We *both* fall.

It's incredibly fast and in slow motion at the same time. My heart's crying out. *Mom! Dad! Help!*

SMACK! We smash into the river below.

We're torn apart. I tumble underwater, crashing, smashing rock, thrashing, flailing, holding my breath.

And *holding it* . . . and *holding it* . . . somersaulting through a cyclone of currents, like a monster's coils trying to hold me under. Me kicking, clawing, trying to reach the surface.

My lungs want to burst. Pinpoints of light explode behind my eyes. I'm about to inhale water, breathe in all the water in the river, when. . . .

I burst out into sunlight.

Air!

I gasp and gag and splutter. I tumble and roll onto my back, twisting and sliding feetfirst down the rapids, bouncing off boulders like a ball in a pinball machine.

The water is so cold my chest seizes. I can't breathe.

I've *got* to breathe!

I cough and shudder and cough again. *Hard!*

My ribs finally loosen. I snag a breath and look around.

What's that downriver? A bundle. A bundle of dark flannel draped over a sweeper.

Dad!

I veer toward him. My soaked clothes are so heavy they almost drag me down.

I fight and kick to keep my head above the surface.

Closer . . . closer now . . . I'm almost there.

Almost there!

I crash feetfirst right beside him and almost get sucked under again. I snatch the dead limb and pull myself up, and hold on.

"*Dad!*" I yell. I fight my way toward him, try to grab hold . . .

. . . but suddenly he's pulled under and away by the river.

He's gone! My hand holds empty air. I can see him bouncing and rolling downriver like a rag doll.

"Dad! Dad!"

NOW WHAT? AND OTHER LIFE-OR-DEATH QUESTIONS

There's nothing I can do but let go. I have to get to Dad.

I let go of the dead limb and let the river take me.

But not completely. I've got to take control—like I would if I were in a kayak or a raft.

But I start to go under. I climb hard, pedaling with my hands and feet, like trying to climb a ladder made of water.

I reach the top. My head pokes out. I breathe. I swing my legs around so I'm gliding feetfirst on my back, kicking off boulders, stumps, river-soaked snags—which reach down into the roiling water like witches trying to snatch me with their bony fingers.

Am I catching up to Dad? I lift my head and look downriver.

I think I see him! The dark flannel. Is it floating? Is Dad floating?

Suddenly I'm pulled underwater again. My lungs cry out for air. I tell myself: *Don't breathe!* But it's a reflex and more than anything in the world right now:

I WANT TO BREATHE!

But if I breathe underwater, I drown.

My brain starts to freeze. It's shutting down. It's getting dark.

But I push hard off the bottom with my feet and pop back up to the surface and breathe! A whole, great, sky full of air.

And there he is.

Dad!

He's pressed against a boulder, his head just barely breaking the surface. The force of the river is pushing against him, pressing, shoving, and now for the first time I see that there's a drop just beyond him, maybe thirty or forty feet.

A cascade! A thundering mist hangs above it.

I roll on my back again, feetfirst, and swerve toward him, swiveling my hands at my hips, like tiny fins or flippers.

BLAM!

I smash into the boulder feetfirst, right beside him.

"Dad!"

His lower lip is in the water. His eyes are shut. He's out cold. It's the pressure of the river, gluing him to the boulder like a postage stamp.

I cling to the boulder with my feet, then throw my arm around his chest and yank with all my might. Pulling left at the same time, toward shore, where I can haul him out.

I kick. I yank.

He moves but is sucked back. Against the boulder.

One last effort.

I *yank!*

Dad slips sideways and I almost lose him. I wrap my arm around his chest again, grab hold of his flannel shirt in my fist, and grip it like a claw.

I kick off. Back into the current. And angle toward shore, flailing with one arm, kicking, my whole body screaming with a fierce animal hunger—

to live!

For both of us to live.

At last my feet hit bottom. I can feel it.

Thank God!

My feet slip. Stones tumble underfoot. The current's like a powerful conveyor belt to hell.

Alone I can make it to shore, but I can't let Dad go. I can't let him go.

His head lolls back. His eyes roll back. He starts to slip under. He's being sucked under. His shirt rips from my hand.

"*NO!*" His face is underwater now. I dip down and try to grab him and lift him back up. Bubbles stream from his nose and mouth.

I'm losing him! I'm losing him! I lift my head out. I grab a handful of his flannel shirt again, and with my other hand grab an overhead branch and pull.

It snaps!

We're both sucked under again. I don't let go of Dad's shirt. We bounce along a gravel bottom and smash feetfirst into a boulder. I swallow water and tumble sideways toward shore, pulling Dad with me. We swirl to the surface in a back eddy, and my feet scramble for the bottom.

I wedge my feet into the bottom. I loop my arm around Dad's chest—and haul his deadweight through the shallows and up the gravelly bank.

We collapse in a dripping heap. But there's no time.

Is he breathing? I look at his chest. It's not moving! His face is blue-gray.

Now my CPR training kicks in. Mom made me get certified when I thought I could make some money babysitting our neighbor's kids. Mom's a nurse and made sure I learned it well.

My heart's pounding like a piston, but I put two shaky fingers to the carotid artery in Dad's throat.

A pulse! *Dad's got a pulse!*

I roll him on his side, wiggle a finger between his lips, and pry his jaws apart. Reddish-brown water spills out. I check to see that he hasn't swallowed his tongue. He hasn't, but I see blood.

I put my ear to his mouth and listen for a breath.

There's no sound! I lay my hand on his chest. It's as still as stone. He's still alive but he must've stopped breathing!

"Dad!" I roll him on his back, pinch his nose, and start doing mouth-to-mouth resuscitation. I try not to panic. I have to try to stay calm. I have to keep breathing into him with strong, steady breaths.

Nothing happens.

I pull away, take another deep breath, and try again.

Suddenly Dad vomits. Blood and water gush into my mouth. I gag and spit it out. I roll him over onto his side again and let the rest spill out.

He's *breathing!* His chest is heaving and he's alive and breathing and spluttering and coughing.

He pulls himself up to his elbows and then collapses. His eyes pop open. They stare at me.

"Dad! You're alive! *Breathe!* Keep breathing!"

Dad's eyes close. I panic. I put my ear to his lips. His

breath tickles my ear. He's just unconscious. He'll be okay, right? He'll come around and we'll go back to the camp and resume our trip. Right?

But what if he doesn't come around? What if his brain is damaged from lack of oxygen?

"Dad! *Wake up!* You have to get up! We have to get you out of here!"

I shake him like a rag doll. A very heavy rag doll. I look around. The Cariboo River races by, oblivious to our plight. Two big black ravens perch on a dead tree. Three more circle high overhead.

"Go away!" I shout. "We're not dead yet!" Don't they wait until your flesh rots? They're not waiting.

"Dad! *Wake up, Dad!*"

His eyes pop open again. He blinks.

He says something. I can't hear it. I put my ear next to his lips. "Aaron?" It comes out in a whispered croak.

I sit bolt upright. "Dad! Geez, you scared me half to death!"

He tries to talk. He can't. He coughs and squeezes his eyes shut and opens them again.

Then he tries to sits up. He can't. Should I help him? I don't know if I should move him. What if he broke his neck, his back?

But I've got to move him. I've got no choice.

When he starts struggling to lift himself again, I give him a hand. I cradle him like a baby.

"I don't . . . feel so good." At least, I think that's what he says. He coughs and spits. Greenish phlegm, streaked red. He tries to take a deep breath, and to clear his throat.

He's having a hard time breathing. He gurgles and wheezes. He lifts his head and forces air into his chest. Then holds his head. "I'm dizzy," he says. "My lungs. . . . My head. . . ." He can't talk anymore. He's in pain.

Now I suddenly realize I hurt all over. I feel like a sack of bruised bones. My left side feels like there's a burning spear in it. My head pounds and my stomach's cramping up on me.

I look down. The knees of my pants are ripped out and the skin is scraped raw. My elbows, too.

Then I feel my lips. They're swollen. I run my tongue over my teeth, and taste blood. I spit it out and run my tongue over my teeth again. I've got a loose tooth, near the front. I can feel it. I wiggle it with my fingers.

I spit, and I'm afraid I spit my tooth out.

No, it's still there. Loose, wiggly, but there.

I look down at my dad.

"Can you stand up, Dad?" Thinking of him, I don't notice my own pain so much.

"No. Not . . . yet," he stammers. He lets his head flop back. I gently lay him on his back. He folds his arms over his chest. He starts shivering, his teeth clack.

I suddenly realize how cold it is. I start shaking too and pull my hoodie off. It weighs a ton. I wring it out and slap it against a boulder.

WHAM! WHAM!

How am I going to get back into that? But all I've got on is a T-shirt. I'm freezing. The canyon's totally in shadow now. It's like a meat locker in here. It's getting late. It's getting dark. We've got to get out of here.

Now.

"We have to go! Come on, Dad, I'll help you up."

He mumbles something but doesn't stir. He lies there like a mummy, arms still crossed over his chest.

What am I going to do?

I wrestle back into my hoodie, then try to lift Dad up.

I can't. Not without his help. "Dad! Get up! We'll freeze down here!"

Dad groans. I cup my hand under his neck and with the other one grab the front of his flannel shirt and manage to pull him into a sitting position.

Then I kneel and snake an arm under his knees and my other arm beneath his shoulders—and *lift!* I get halfway up when he slides off, but he lands on his feet and I hold him upright. He sways and leans all his weight into me.

"Come on, Dad. Here, we'll walk together. You can do it!" With one arm gripping him tight I take a step. He staggers forward. I take another step. He lurches and almost falls, but stays up, and takes another shaky step.

"Awesome!" I say. And together we stumble like drunks across the stones and downfall trees along the river, our wet shoes squelching with each step.

In this fashion—sometimes falling but always getting back up—we finally get to the bottom of the waterfall. It's almost dark now. We stop and Dad slumps down toward the ground, but I keep hauling him back up. I look up at the steep winding path along the falls. The slippery, moss-covered stones.

Suddenly his knees give out completely and he slumps to the ground in a heap. He lies there at my feet, like a load of laundry. A wet, heavy load.

I look up: switchbacks, the long steep path to the top in the dark.

Now what?

THE LAST MATCH

The more I look up at the path beside the waterfall the more I realize Dad can't walk up it, even leaning against me. It's too dangerous. If one of us slips, we'd both topple back into the raging cauldron below.

I have to think. But there's no time for thinking. But I have to think anyway. The path is dark, but I see a glow through the trees above, up on the edge of the canyon.

It must be the moon. It should be almost full by now. Dad says something. I can't make out what he's saying over the roar of the waterfall.

"Louder, Dad!" I bend my head down near his mouth.

"You go. I can't . . . walk. Go get . . . help."

"No way! I'm not leaving you down here. You're coughing up blood. You'll freeze." He'd attract some hungry grizzlies for sure, but I don't say that out loud. "Just let me think a minute."

We haven't seen anybody else the whole trip, not a soul. Just one canoe broken in half. Other paddlers should be coming behind us in a day or two, but we don't have a day or two. Dad won't make it that long. Rangers are supposed to patrol periodically, but we haven't seen even one. It's probably not worth their while if it's just a few of us paddling the circuit now. We're registered at the ranger station, but Dad estimated we'd be back in eight or nine days. It's only been six. They won't start missing us for a few days.

We can't wait that long. We have to get out now. I *have* to find a way.

Just then the moon breaks free of the trees and shines down on us, and I don't know why, but suddenly I know what to do. What I *have* to do.

I take some deep breaths and say, "Dad, we're going now. It's time to go."

I hunch down and slide my arm and shoulder beneath him, plant my legs and feet into the ground like a weight-lifter . . .

. . . and I *lift!!* I mean, I lift him clear off the ground! And into a fireman's carry—slung sideways across my shoulders.

Dad's taller than me and outweighs me by at least twenty pounds, but thinking of Cassidy carrying my dad up out of Desolation Canyon two years ago gives me a shot of pure energy. Superhuman strength.

Still, I creak under his weight and I feel like I'm going to snap in two. But feeling that energy coursing through me, I keep waddling in a half crouch, and start slowly, very slowly, up the path.

One step at a time.

I climb through a cloud of mist, the roar of the waterfall, with Dad on my back, across my shoulders—dangling, deadweight, huffing, groaning, but not saying anything. Wheezing.

First one switchback, then another. Up and up. Endlessly up and up and up.

After a few minutes, exhaustion starts taking its toll, but it's also taking the chill out of my bones. I'm sweating. I'm soaked. Sweat, river water, spray from the waterfall.

I don't know if I can keep going. I need to stop and rest. But I'm afraid that if I put Dad down, I won't be able to lift him back up.

So I keep taking one step, and then another, and another.

I'm gasping. My heart is thumping, pounding, in my chest, in my ears. My thigh muscles are burning, my calves. My knees and hips are straining, tearing, aching.

I keep trudging with my load up the hill. And then I remember that dream I had. The grizzly bear carrying the moon up the mountain. The Moon Bear. Almost making it to the top.

Then falling, tumbling back down the mountain with the moon.

And starting up all over again.

But I can't fall. I can't tumble down the mountain. I can't start all over again. I have to keep going. Keep climbing. Up and up. Up toward the sky.

Finally, just when I think I'm going to die, I see the top of the path. Another fifty yards. Half the length of a football field.

But farther, really. Much farther. Because of the switch-backs.

But I keep going. Seeing the top sparks hope. Hope that I will make it. I will make it. I will make it.

And at last, *I make it!*

We make it!

We make it to the top of the canyon and I lower myself down to all fours, then slowly swing Dad around and let him slide slowly to the ground.

I flop beside him, sprawled out, gasping. My chest heaving. I close my eyes and see stars. I open them, and see stars, dimmed a bit by the rising moon. It's getting close to full.

Suddenly Dad coughs. An awful, ragged cough. He tries to sit up and gags. He tries to clear his throat. He launches into an attack of coughing.

I roll him on his side, patting his back.

We have to get going. The dampness and chill are creeping back into my bones. Dad must be freezing. We're both wet.

And hungry. Hunger's like a fish hook tugging my guts.

And the more we wait here the hungrier we will get. The colder we'll get.

I take several deep breaths. I rub my legs and shake my arms and roll my head around, and try to loosen my shoulders. And take more deep breaths.

Then I say, "Up we go, Dad. It's a bummer, but we've got to go."

Again, I sneak my arm beneath him, my shoulder. First I lean him against a boulder. Then I sink into a deep squat and heft him onto my shoulders and lift. With all my might, I lift.

We're up. I almost fall backwards. I catch myself. I start along the path.

One step at a time.

When we start descending I figure it'll be easier now. But my knees keep buckling beneath me. It's easier on my lungs, but even harder on my legs.

Thinking of fish and a fire, I get a second wind. I try to think of gravity as my friend. Along with gravity, my friend, we are climbing down now. Down.

I think of Cassidy. He carried my dad up the walls of Desolation Canyon, but two or three of us helped get Dad back down.

Now it's just me. And gravity. A tricky friendship.

There's less than half a mile to go.

It's the longest half mile in the world.

I round a bend and finally see the moonlit lake below. Dad's dangling arms and legs are swinging with each step I take.

I think he's gone unconscious again. I fall into a kind of stupor from exhaustion, but I don't let go. I swing my legs and stumble along, like a dying but loyal beast of burden.

Time disappears. One leg shuffles in front of the other. Down and down and down we go.

One step at a time. Until . . .

The lake the lake! We're at the lake!

I don't stop. I can't stop. We have to get back to our camp. Fifty yards to go. Forty yards. Twenty.

At last, I strain with my last ounce of strength and lower my dad next to the fire ring. We both collapse on the cold ground. I'm totally exhausted. And dehydrated. I need water, but I can't move.

And Dad, he's out. He's out cold. I want to get him out of his wet clothes and into a sleeping bag, but I don't know how I'm going to do that. I want to drink water and make a fire and catch a fish and eat. Especially eat. And feed my father.

Wanting isn't the same as doing.

I've got to *do* this.

I shake myself awake and glug some water from my water bottle and try to think. We *have* to eat. We *have* to get dry. And warm. We *have* to rest. To sleep.

A cold wind blows down from the mountains. I have to try to get a big fire going. *Now!*

First I pull Dad's sleeping bag out of our tent and over to the fire pit. I fluff it out next to Dad, and roll him on it, then pull it closed over him. I lift his head and stick his small pillow beneath it. I'll have to get his wet clothes off him later, after I get the fire going. No time now.

Luckily there's a small stack of firewood leftover from before. With the moon and stars as my only light, I set a few of the slenderest pieces into a little tepee, with some birch or aspen bark—whatever, it's like stiff but brittle paper—shred it into a fire nest, then twist the last of our newspaper and stuff it underneath.

Dad had left the four remaining matches in an empty tin

of mints, in the tent, and I get it.

I kneel by the fire and I think to myself, Okay, here goes!

And I strike the first match against a large, rough stone.

The head flies off. Bummer!

Three matches left.

I try striking this match less forcefully, but nothing happens. I keep trying till the head is worn down to a nub. To nothing.

Two. *Two* matches left! Dad groans. I check him out but he's still out cold. The moon is high overhead. The night is bright and clear and cold.

Okay. *This is the one!* I *will* the match to light, and with fumbling fingers, scratch it across the stone.

It breaks in half! My heart breaks with it.

I feel like giving up, but I'm obsessed with getting this fire started.

I'm obsessed. I put all my concentration into the last match.

The last match!

I focus on it with all the power of the universe funneled down to this one match.

And strike.

It flares up!

And goes out!

A whiff of smoke spirals into nothingness.

SAVING DAD

NOOOO!"

I jump up and curse and pull my hair. I drop back to my knees and pound my fist into the stone. I'm so freaked I don't even feel the pain.

I'm frantic. I'm pacing around talking to myself. No food. No fire. No warmth. No hope.

I'm shivering now, but I don't know if it's from the cold or my raging frustration.

I suddenly get this image in my head. Brian in that book by Gary Paulsen. *Hatchet.* He's alone in the wilderness with no matches, no lighter, just a hatchet. He strikes it against stone to make sparks to start a fire.

But we don't have a hatchet!

Dad knew there'd be firewood at the campsites, so he didn't bring one. Smart, Dad. Now we'll just starve out here and become bear food, picked clean by crows and ravens.

But wait!

Wait!

The second to last match. It broke in half!

I drop to my knees and scrabble around like a starving beaver. I've got to find that wooden match, the half with the head still attached.

I can't find it.

I've *got* to find it.

I scurry around in the moonlight, in the starlight, my nose almost to the ground, like a dog.

I find it!

No! It's the wrong half! The other half should be around here somewhere. Right?

There it is! In a patch of dirt surrounded by low ground-cover. Lit slightly by a ray of moonlight.

I snatch it up like a gold nugget, and squat back down over the fire ring. I hold the match at its end, an inch or so from the head. I try to steady my hand. I'm shivering and shaking all over, but I've got to calm down. I've got to strike this with the precision of a brain surgeon.

I take a deep breath and force myself to calm down. *I can do this. I can do this.*

At least, I think I can.

The moon seems to hang in suspension.

I take a deep breath—holding the stub of a match a hair's breadth above the boulder—and strike. . . .

It flairs up! It burns my fingers. I almost drop it.

But I don't. I lower it slowly to the tip of twisted paper, holding my breath.

Presto!

A tiny flame blooms—and it's enough! It eats into the edge of twisted paper and I cup it from the wind.

"Ouch!" Flames reach up and bite my fingers. I pull my hand away and spit on them. I can smell singed flesh but there's no time to run to the lake and soak my fingers. I've got to keep the fire going.

I gently coax it along with my breath. First the shredded bark catches fire, and then flames crawl along the sides of one piece of firewood, and another, and I gradually blow harder and harder till finally the fire's blazing.

"Dad! Look! I got a fire going!" But Dad's still out. "Dad, wake up! A fire!" Dad doesn't stir, but I decide that's a good thing. He needs to sleep. And he's near the fire.

But I have to get him out of his wet clothes.

I open up the sleeping bag and wrestle him out of his jacket first, then I peel off his shirt, take off his sandals, and finally tug off his pants. It's like grappling with a 150-pound rag doll!

And through the whole wrestling match he doesn't wake up. That can't be good.

Then I zip him back inside the bag and tuck his pillow back under his head.

Now I feed the flames with more and more firewood, until eventually a bonfire's roaring in the night. I admire it for about one minute, and decide it's time to go fishing.

But first I tear off my hoodie and hang it over a pine branch near the fire, to dry. Then I strip off my T-shirt and hang it next to my hoodie. They drip in the moonlight. I don't have another pair of jeans, just cutoffs and it's too cold for those. And I only have the one pair of shoes, my soggy river sandals, so I have to slog around half wet while I dry off with a towel and rifle through our wet bags for shirts. All I've got are dirty T-shirts. I layer on three smelly T-shirts and put on a torn windbreaker over them. I'm still freezing my butt off, but it'll have to do.

I quickly rig up my rod and check on Dad again. He's snoring, his face glowing in the firelight. With his filthy face and whiskers, and his ratty hair, he looks like a bum who's given up on life.

But I know he's not a bum. He tried to save my life.

He tried to save my life! Can you believe that? And almost lost his own life doing it.

So I'm gonna catch him a fish. A prize rainbow. And I'm gonna cook it up and say, *Here, Dad. For you!*

I stroll off along a path through the woods. I think my chances will be best where a creek flows into the lake, a hundred yards away. I come around the bend just as something crosses my path and freezes.

A lynx!

I stop in my tracks and stay absolutely still. I've seen bobcats a few times but this is much bigger, much longer legs, with tufts of fur on its ears and huge paws.

I stare at it. It stares at me. Its eyes in the moonlight burn with a golden fire.

I snap its picture with my mind's camera, and the lynx springs off into the dark forest.

The moment's over, but I'll carry it with me for the rest of my life. A snapshot from the wild. A snapshot from the day my dad tried to save my life, and I ended up saving Dad.

At the creek I look at the moonlight on the lake. It's awesome. It's a rippling gold path leading right toward me. I cast my lure into it and start reeling it in.

It feels like I'm casting for the moon.

Almost instantly, my rod jerks and dances in my hands, then bends over till the tip almost touches the water. It feels like a big one! I loosen the drag so the line won't snap, and watch a slippery muscle of light leap out of the lake and plunge back in. I let it jig and jag, rise, and dance on the water, and plunge back in. Then I start reeling it in again.

It's twenty feet away.

Ten.

I see its tail swish the surface, and then I realize:

I didn't bring the net!

If I try pulling it out of the water without a net, it might flip off the hook and get away.

I tighten the drag and prop the rod in the fork of a stunted tree and scramble into the lake after it. It darts and swirls and I snatch at it with both hands before it can snap the line, or tear the hook from its lips.

It squirts through my hands like a bar of soap. I grab the line with one hand, lift my foot, and wrap the line around my leg. Then I lunge for the fish with all the hungry energy of a grizzly bear.

"Gotcha!" I grasp it, as if with claws, and fling it out onto the shore, like a grizzly would.

A rainbow trout, its scales gleaming in the moonlight.

I slosh out of the water after it. It flips and flops on the ground. It's a big trout, well over a foot long. Its gills work in and out, in and out. It flaps on its side, one eye staring at me. I pick up a rock and knock the fish on the head to put it out of its misery.

It's not until now that I realize that two fingers on my left hand sting as if they'd been lashed with the tendrils of a jellyfish.

My burnt fingers. A fish I caught for my dad. My dad whose life I saved. A fire I made with the last half of the last match.

Okay. Now I think it's okay if I feel a little pride.

And I do.

HANG ON!

'm worried about Dad.

I keep waking up to listen to his breathing. It still doesn't sound good. When I don't hear any breathing at all, I have a momentary panic. But then he catches his breath like he's gagging, and I worry that he's going to choke to death on blood or water or both.

I roll Dad on his side, and try to go back to sleep.

I can't. I listen to the mournful howl of a lone wolf in the distance. If I had the energy, I'd howl back.

Last night I rushed back to camp with just the one fish because I was afraid to leave Dad alone even a minute longer.

When I got back, triumphantly carrying my trout, he was on his hands and knees, coughing and choking, and spitting up blood. He had managed to get into some dry clothes. The fire had dwindled but was still going strong.

I knelt at his side, dangling the fish. "Look, Dad! Look what I caught!"

He waved it away and sagged back on the ground. Then he looked up and grinned. "That's a beaut, Aaron." First words he'd said to me in hours—I was grateful to hear them.

"Now we can eat, Dad!"

"You eat it. I don't think I can keep it down."

"But you've got to eat. Here, I'm gonna grill this baby up real good." I dangled it in front of his eyes. "Check it out. How sweet is that?"

I didn't bother to clean the trout. I was in too much of a hurry to feed my dad, and myself. I just plopped the fish on the grill over the fire and fed the fire till the trout cooked on one side, then I flipped it over and cooked it on the other side.

The hunger had been there all along, but now, with the wonderful smell of the trout, crackling and sizzling on the open fire, the emptiness in my belly *screamed* for food.

When the skin on the fish was good and crispy, I served Dad first.

But Dad wouldn't eat. He kept telling me I should eat. Finally, I helped lean him against the boulder, and I fed him like a baby, one forkful at a time. "Open wide, Dad! Open wide!"

After awhile he said, "No more, Aaron. I can't." He rolled back down to the ground and closed his eyes.

I ate what was left, a little over half. I peeled the skin back and picked the flesh off with my fingers, tasting every morsel, memorizing the flavor as if this would be my last meal.

Then I ate the crispy skin. Kinda like fishy potato chips, but yummier than it sounds. I stared down at the eyeballs.

I still couldn't do it. Instead, I picked up the whole head and tossed it as hard as I could into the lake.

An offering for the fish. *Thanks, fish!*

Then I cleaned everything up. I didn't want a bear coming in the night.

I picked up one end of his sleeping bag and pulled Dad along the ground, back to the front of the tent. I decided to build up the fire in the hopes that it would still be going in the morning.

So I had to go out and search in the moonlight for dry kindling. I came back with mostly damp kindling, which I stacked up next to the fire to dry, and to use during the night and in the morning.

By the time I got to the tent, Dad had managed to crawl inside on his own. He was snuggled deep in his bag, just his nose sticking out.

I thought of fishing right from shore for tomorrow's breakfast, but I was too exhausted. I managed to wiggle out of my clothes, and I think I fell asleep before my head even hit the pillow.

* * *

But now it's the middle of night and I can't get back to sleep. Dad's breathing is ragged. Tomorrow I've got to get Dad some help. Good thing we've been traveling in a circle, so we're almost back to where we started. By midday tomorrow we should be able to reach the small ranger station at Babcock Creek. And the main ranger station where we began this crazy trip is maybe a half day beyond that. At least according to the map. I don't think Dad can make it through another night like this.

And we've used the last match. The last *half* of a match.

So what are we going to do? How am I going to get him into the kayak? And if I get him in, what if he slouches over sideways, unconscious? What if he falls out, or capsizes the boat, or both?

What if?

And if I remember right, there are at least two portages left. How are we going to do that?

My mind's spinning in circles. My burnt fingers are on fire; they're blistered, the hairs singed off. I still hurt all over from bouncing off boulders, and my stomach is an emptiness aching to be filled.

But I have to sleep. I *have* to. I'll need every ounce of energy for tomorrow.

If we don't make it out tomorrow, we might not make it out at all.

I get up and feed the fire, then crawl back into my bag

I *will* myself to sleep. I count backwards from a hundred. I drift off. I wake up. I drift off. If I have any dreams I can't remember them.

* * *

In the morning there's no question of me fishing. The fire's gone out. And there's no time.

Dad's worse. *Way worse.*

I fight against a rising panic. I feel like I'm in a wild current and it's taking me where it wants to go.

Maybe over a waterfall.

I've got to take control. I've got to move faster than the current.

There's a thick white fog, shrouding the world. I rip my hoodie down off the branch I'd left it hanging on, and a few pinecones come down with it.

Pine nuts! Mom uses them to cook with sometimes. And if squirrels can eat them, maybe I can too. I jump up and shake the limb as hard as I can. Cones rain down, but no nuts pop out. Maybe they're the wrong kind of cones, or it's the wrong time of year.

Whatever, there's no time to try and dig pine nuts out of the cones. We'll just have to go hungry.

I run back to the tent, but I can't take it down with Dad still inside. "Dad! Are you awake?" I crawl inside and shake him. He groans. "Dad! Wake up! We have to go. *Now!*"

I pull him outside still in his bag, and break down the tent. There's no time to let the dew dry. I pack everything and stow the wet bags in the holds. I'm running. Everything I do now is at a run.

Dad finally wakes and sits up. He's stupefied. Groggy. I don't think he even knows where we are. "Dad. We're going now. We're going in the kayak. We're going home, Dad."

"Home?" Dad rubs a hand down his face. His eyes are bloodshot. His hair's poking out every which way, wet with sweat. He looks like a newly born chick, dazed by the light.

I stuff his bag and practically drag him to the kayak, then have to lift him and swing him feetfirst into the cockpit. He sits there, totally lost. I tell him not to lean sideways. To slouch down as much as he can, his legs as deep as possible in the leg space, and to just hold on.

I don't even try to get him into a spray skirt. I push his paddle down into the leg space beside him, and tell him to loop one arm around it. I think of harnessing him to the kayak with the bowline or the belts, but decide against it. Too dangerous. If the boat capsizes he'd be trapped.

I take one more look at the campsite, then climb in and shove off. I'm a pro at this now. We ease out through the reeds, and then I start paddling—for the both of us.

The fog encloses us. It's so thick and the air's so still, it feels like everything in the world is muffled. But I get the sense that we're being watched. That we're being followed. I think of the lynx last night, the grizzly the night before. There's something out there, watching, waiting. Something big is going to happen today. I can *feel* it. It could be the end of everything.

Or some kind of new beginning.

It's a good thing I got oriented last night when I went

fishing. Today I follow the shoreline till we flow back into the Cariboo River. From Unna Lake it's a quarter of a mile paddle—*upstream!* Back toward the falls!

Solo!

It's almost impossible. But I've got to do it. I've *got* to.

"Hang on, Dad! It might get bumpy!" I hunker over and dig in. I use my whole body with each stroke. I push against the double-bladed paddle with one hand and pull with the other. I discover that if I hug the inside bend of the shore, the strain of the current is less.

But when I try to cross the river to turn into Babcock Creek, the current starts sucking us back downstream.

"*Whoa!*" The current's hitting us broadside. It's driving so hard against the bottom of our kayak it almost tips us over toward the upstream side. I yell, "Lean away from the current, Dad! Lean downstream!"

Then I realize, Dad's unconscious. He *can't* lean downstream. He's slumped in the cockpit in front of me.

I touch his shoulder with the tip of my paddle. He needs to be awake, aware.

I yell, "Wake up, Dad! Wake up!"

The kayak is tipping. It's tipping.

"Hang on, Dad! *HANG ON!*"

A SIGNAL FROM THE WILD

Dad's suddenly alert! He leans away from the current and we both brace our paddles—flat out on the surface—at the same time!

It saves us! Without his help, I think we would've gone over.

I *know* we would have gone over!

Now all I have do is angle the nose above the creek, which I can barely make out in the fog, and paddle like our lives depend on it.

Our lives *do* depend on it! And after a crazy mad churn across the powerful current, I'm able to turn us up into Babcock Creek.

And it's just in the nick of time! Dad loses his grip on the paddle and it slips into the suds, but I snatch it up before it can be sucked downstream.

I hand it back to him, but I can see he's all played out now. He lays his paddle across the hull and scoots back down deep into his seat.

Just up Babcock Creek we see the small ranger hut shrouded in fog. There's a slip for the ranger's boats but there aren't any boats in sight. I pull in and tell Dad to just stay put, and I go up to check out the hut.

It's locked. There's nobody around. In fact, it looks like no one's been here for a while, maybe all winter. There are cobwebs in the window. I think of leaving a note but I'm in a hurry and I don't think it would do any good, anyway. Who knows how long it will be until a ranger gets here?

Dad's in bad shape and seems to be getting worse by the minute. Without fire, without medical attention, I don't know if he could make it through another night.

I have to get him back to the main ranger station on Bowron Lake, where we started.

Today!

When I get back, Dad's asleep or unconscious, I can't tell which. I slip his paddle in beside him and loop his arm around it. He doesn't stir. "Hang in there, Dad," I say, and we slide back off into the thick white mist.

There's a sign saying to pull out and portage. Babcock Creek's supposed to be too shallow to kayak, but it's high now with spring runoff and I decide to keep paddling as long as I can.

But at one point the kayak scrapes bottom. There must be a big deposit of sand here. I have to climb out of the kayak and line us through the reedy shallows. I think of an old movie my parents like to watch: *The African Queen.*

Humphrey Bogart has to wade down a jungle-clogged channel, towing this old-time boat, the *African Queen*, and his whole body gets covered with leeches. He totally freaks.

I hope the water here's too cold for leeches.

It's not! When the creek's deep enough, I climb back into the kayak and find half a dozen leeches stuck to my skin. Bloodsuckers! *Gross!* A few have crawled up beneath my pants legs and are clamped onto my calves!

I pull at them, their huge mouths glued to me, stretching my skin with each yank.

Splop! Blood smears my legs. *Eeeeew!* I toss the slimy creatures into the water, and start paddling.

We've wasted way too much time! Dad's stirring now. He's coughing again, hawking blood-soaked phlegm over the side.

"You okay, Dad?"

"Aye aye, skipper. Full steam ahead!"

I can't believe I heard him right. He hasn't called me "skipper" since I was a little kid. Skipper means captain.

And captain I am. We wind through the last of Babcock Creek and burst into Babcock Lake. It's still foggy, but it's beginning to lift in places. Dad mumbles that maybe he can help paddle now, but his voice sounds weak, and I tell him to just take it easy and rest.

He paddles anyway, but he's too slow. Our paddles clash. "Relax, Dad! It's all good. Just kick back—but hang on to your paddle!"

We hear a loon call. Across the lake another loon calls back.

I paddle toward the sound of the loon, and see it take off—first running on the water—as I paddle into the shallows of the far shore.

We have four lakes to go: Skoi, Spectacle, Swan, and Bowron. Two of those lakes are attached, which means just two easy portages left, both short and not too steep.

That's a good thing because when we start the portage to Skoi Lake, Dad can't walk. Every time he tries his knees buckle beneath him. I think he's totally drained. All he's had to eat in the last couple of days is a few bites of fish.

Me too, but so what? I'm wrestling with some demon and I'm winning. I think. *I hope.* I remember the dream of the grizzly—the beast—and the smell of his breath right behind me. And I remember the dream of the Moon Bear, pushing the moon up the mountain. Yeah, I know how he feels.

We walk just a few yards when I say, "Okay, Dad. Take a rest."

He slides down to the ground and in a minute he's out cold again. I decide to leave the kayak and come back for it later. I squat down and hoist Dad over my shoulders in a fireman's carry and stagger along the trail, his arms and legs swinging, his body bending toward earth.

At Skoi Lake, I lean him gently against the trunk of an aspen tree and plop down beside him. We're both exhausted,

but at least Dad's conscious now. I catch my breath and start to stand up. Dad grabs my arm. I sit back down and look at him. He stares right into my eyes but doesn't say a word.

But he says more in that silence than he has all trip.

I break the silence. "You're a tough old man, Dad."

He says, "You're a tough young man, Aaron." He still holds my eyes with his.

He pats my arm. I stand back up.

"Don't go running off, Dad. I'll be back in a few." I jog back off up the portage trail and let the look in his eyes sink in. The warmth there. The love. The gratitude. Whatever you want to call it.

It's only about a quarter of a mile back to retrieve the kayak. I jog the whole way there. I think if I stop I'll just collapse and never get back up.

I pull the cart with the kayak by myself. Slow but steady.

My muscles burn. Everything hurts. But I'm not complaining. There's nobody to complain to.

In fact, in a weird way, I feel almost happy.

* * *

I paddle us across tiny, tree-lined Skoi Lake. Tatters of fog hang from the trees. I hear the slap of a beaver tail and the *caw! caw!* of curious crows.

We repeat the whole process between Skoi Lake and Spectacle/Swan Lakes (which are attached)—me carrying Dad, then running back to haul the kayak.

All along the way I search for something to eat. But it's too early in the year here for ripe berries. It's too early for most things. There are some mushrooms but I don't know what's poisonous and what's not. And there's no time to stop and look for food, anyway.

I'm so hungry I could eat a tree of fire! I said that when I was three or four. Dad wrote it down, along with some other things I said, and sent the lines as a poem to a kid's magazine. It was published! I guess that was the beginning of my writing career.

Before we set off across Spectacle Lake, I slump against a tree beside my dad. Just for a minute. Just to catch my breath. I'm about to stand back up when something comes crashing through the trees and into the lake. Not fifty feet away.

A mother moose and her calf. They splash through the

shallows, wheezing and huffing, and start swimming, their tongues hanging out, their legs churning.

And right behind them is a huge grizzly! He ignores us and plunges in and plows through the water. He's gaining on them as they round a sandy point and out of our sight.

As if it's a signal from the wild, I leap up and pull Dad up with me. We have to get out of here. I manage to wrestle Dad into the kayak and start paddling like mad.

He's slumped down in the cockpit again. I think he's unconscious. That's okay. I've got my own rhythm and nothing's going to stop me now. Not hunger. Not exhaustion. Not the weather.

I paddle as if a grizzly's on my tail.

My arms are killing me. My back feels broken. My stomach is twisted into knots. But I can't stop. My sole purpose in life is to paddle hard.

Spectacle Lake is long. It's endless. It's one continuous blur of fatigue.

At a narrow S-shaped bend Spectacle becomes Swan Lake—and I keep paddling. I don't slow down. The sun is getting lower. Dad's still out cold.

My stomach is eating itself. My hunger is a drum and I paddle to the beat. My hands are tough from a week of paddling or they'd be a mass of bloody blisters by now.

Blisters. Red boils cover the two small fingers on my left hand where I burned them. I've been moving so fast I've hardly noticed.

We finally enter Bowron River, which will take us to the last of the lakes: Bowron Lake. A strong current helps us as we snake through the shallow wetland. Waterfowl prowl the tall sedge grass.

Three-quarters of an hour later and we make it to Bowron Lake! Park headquarters, where we started this trip an eternity ago and where our car is parked, is just across the lake.

I check the map: 7.2 kilometers to go! Just a little over four miles!

We can do this! *We can do this!* Dad, wake up! No, don't! Just stay low. Let me take you home!

We're less than halfway across the lake when the wind picks up. We hit chop. Little whitecaps. The wind wakes Dad and he sits up and looks around. The sun is almost down. He grabs his paddle but holds it across his lap. He coughs a few times and swallows

Something's coming. We both feel it. It's coming behind us and it sounds like a train roaring through a tunnel. Or a bear roaring down a canyon.

It's the wind!

Are you kidding me? We're almost home and now I've got a windstorm to deal with?

I paddle to outrace the wind. To outrace the beast breathing down my neck. The grizzly.

And that's when it hits me.

I am the grizzly. I am my own worst enemy.

Not Dad. Not the principal. Not my teachers.

Me!

I can be my worst enemy or I can be my own best friend. It's up to me. I can be the Moon Bear carrying the moon. Like I carried Dad. Me. Aaron. Trying. Failing.

Succeeding.

With that thought, I'm a windmill of churning energy. Dad steadies us by bracing his paddle down against the surface with each surge.

He's the balancer.

Suddenly we're surfing on the windblown waves!

"Wahoo!" I howl. I whoop and holler—

. . . until over the roar of the wind and the water we can hear the roar of something else.

A motor.

It's a flat-bottomed jet boat, coming toward us from the dock at the end of Bowron Lake, less than four hundred yards away! The boat circles around us as the pilot throttles the motor down to a low gurgle.

"Need some help?" It's Pam, the ranger! She swipes the billowing red hair from her face and smiles.

"Naw, we're good!" I shout, and raise my fist in triumph.

We're back. *We did it!* Beaten but not beat.

Alive!

Just then Dad swivels around, raises his fist—and almost flips us over. "Oops!" he says, and laughs.

There's nothing to do but laugh back.

EPILOGUE

We spent one night at Pam's little house, eating good home cooking, me writing like crazy in my journal and then sleeping for like fourteen hours. In the morning Dad insisted he could drive.

He'd spent a lot of time using Pam's computer and on his phone, but he wouldn't tell me why. Very mysterious.

The doctor at the medical clinic in Quesnel, about sixty miles from Bowron Lakes, checked Dad out. Dad's ribs were bruised and he'd bitten his tongue badly, and he'd gotten water in his lungs. He was lucky he didn't get pneumonia, but he was suffering from exposure, dehydration, and exhaustion. They wanted to observe him overnight, but he wanted to "hit the road." They told us to rest and to eat well and to drink lots of fluids.

Especially Dad. I was actually feeling good. Good about myself. Good about everything. While I'd waited at the clinic I brought my journal up to date. And I was getting an idea for the story.

It had to do with a King (my dad). And the Moon Bear (me).

I had a lot of the story sketched out, I just needed an ending.

* * *

Now it's a day and a half later, in the Kootenay region of the Canadian Rockies. We drove down to Kimberly, not far north of eastern Washington and northern Idaho, and when we pull up in front of the Alpine Resort—I get the surprise of my life.

There's Lisa and Roger and good-ol' bad-ol' Cassidy, leaning against a pickup truck! Their arms are folded, their faces are blank, and they look like they're just, well, hangin'.

Then they burst into great big smiles.

I jump out of our car and yell, "What's up?"

Cassidy points. I look. It's a snowy peak in the distance. Dad climbs out of our car and says, "Grizzly Peak, Aaron. It's the closest one I could find on such short notice."

"*WHAAAAT?* But how—?"

Lisa cuts in. "Aren't you even gonna say hi, Aaron?" She opens her arms wide. "Hey," I say. We hug. I don't want to let go.

I can't believe this! Any of it!

Cassidy says, "Hey, bro! I heard you carried your dad up some waterfall or something. Can you carry him up *that?*" He points at Grizzly Peak again. "Because if you can't, I *can.*"

He pounds his chest, and grins.

Roger hugs Dad, then me. "Are we ready to roll, mates? I don't have all day."

So this is what Dad was up to. He'd Googled Grizzly Peak—turns out there are Grizzly Peaks all over the western US and Canada, too—then arranged to have everybody meet us here. Everybody but Willie. He couldn't get away from work. Cassidy had a river guide job set up for the day after next, not four hours away! How crazy is that? Roger and Lisa took a long weekend and drove clear up from Grants Pass, Oregon, driving until late last night, then starting out early this morning.

"You did this for *me?*" I asked.

"*He* did it for you," said Roger, nodding toward my dad. "For what you did for him."

* * *

Now we've been climbing Grizzly Peak for the last three hours, taking it slow and easy. One step at a time. The first part's just a gradual hike up the mountainside, below the snowline. But now we're at the foot of the final assault on the peak. From here, it's a hard steep climb up rock and scree, through snow and ice, and the wind's howling around us like wolves. A few shredded clouds whip by. It's not that high a mountain, but high enough. Dad's breathing hard. We're all sweating in the cold air.

I look around. There are no grizzlies here. It's just Dad

and me, and my good friends, Lisa, Roger, and Cassidy. A wilderness reunion, of sorts.

Beyond Grizzly Peak there are other peaks and ranges of mountains going all the way up into Alaska, and down through the mountain states and into Mexico.

But right now there's just this one peak. Rock and ice against the deep blue sky, the cold wind swirling around in little snow devils.

It's getting late. The moon will be full tonight. If we make the peak, we'll be climbing back down in the moonlight.

After a short rest I say, "Okay. I can do this, Dad, if you can."

"I know you can," Dad says. "You lead the way, Aaron. I'll be right behind you."

And that's when I get the idea for the ending:

Atop Grizzly Peak, the bear became me, and the moon floated up into the sky where it belonged.

DISCUSSION QUESTIONS

1. *In the beginning of the story, Aaron is expelled for bringing a pocketknife to school. Consider the school's zero tolerance policy. Write a persuasive argument for why you think Aaron should or should not be expelled (or suspended) for the knife incident. Cite evidence from the story as well as outside evidence to support your position.* (CCSS.ELA-LITERACY.CCRA.R.8, CCSS.ELA-LITERACY.CCRA.W.1)

2. *How is this adventure different from Aaron's previous trips with his dad to Bella Bella and Desolation Canyon? Why do you think the author chose to include those differences? Cite passages from the text to support your opinions.* (CCSS.ELA-LITERACY.CCRA.R.9)

3. *During his adventure, Aaron sees many different animals that make him pause to think or change his actions. Pick one of those encounters, and rewrite the scene from the animal's*

point of view. How does the change in perspective affect the tone and purpose of the story? (CCSS.ELA-LITERACY.CCRA.R.6)

4. *Aaron talks about freedom several times in the story. What does freedom mean to Aaron, and why do you think it's important to him at this point in his life?* (CCSS.ELA-LITERACY.CCRA.R.4)

5. *The author of* Grizzly Peak *frequently uses metaphors and similes to enrich the story.*

   Examples:
   - *". . . paddle like demons."*
   - *"It's as if the rain gods have turned off a celestial spigot."*
   - *". . . the moon growing fat, like a piñata filled with candy."*

6. *Find additional examples in the book. Explain what the author is trying to say with each metaphor or simile.* (CCSS.ELA-LITERACY.CCRA.R.4)

7. *On page 73, Dad says, "Some dreams become real. . . . They become who you are. They reflect your fears, your wishes." What do you think the author means by that?* (CCSS.ELA-LITERACY.CCRA.R.1)

8. *Aaron's dad talks about wanting to be a jazz pianist, while Aaron wants to be a rapper. How are the two styles of music*

similar according to the text? How are they different? Listen to examples from each genre to help you better understand the comparison. (CCSS.ELA-LITERACY.CCRA.R.7)

9. *In what ways (if any) would the story have been different if Aaron had taken this journey with someone other than his father? How would the action and underlying tension have been affected if his kayaking partner had been someone he didn't know well, like a counselor or a river guide? How would that have affected the message of the story?*
(CCSS.ELA-LITERACY.CCRA.R.3)

10. *Why does being captain matter to Aaron? How does this relate to his life outside of this adventure? Cite details from the story to support your response.* (CCSS.ELA-LITERACY.CCRA.R.4)

11. *What does it mean when Aaron thinks, "I am the Grizzly" as he paddles away from the windstorm on the last lake?*
(CCSS.ELA-LITERACY.CCRA.R.4)

12. *How is Grizzly Peak similar to another book you've read? Cite examples from both books to support your comparison.*
(CCSS.ELA-LITERACY.CCRA.R.9)

13. *Read either* Desolation Canyon *or* Bella Bella, *stories about Aaron's other two wilderness adventures with his dad. How has Aaron's character developed over the course of these*

stories? How has he changed? Do you find this latest Aaron
more or less relatable than who he was in the earlier books?
Give examples from both texts to support your answer.
(CCSS.ELA-LITERACY.CCRA.R.3)

14. *What scene would you consider the climax of this story?*
    Give details from the book to help support your choice.
    (CCSS.ELA-LITERACY.CCRA.R.5)

15. *The characters in this story survive many difficult challenges,*
    both physical and emotional. Describe one obstacle a charac-
    ter overcomes in this story. Include details from the book
    about the problem and how it was solved.
    (CCSS.ELA-LITERACY.CCRA.R.1)

16. *Why did the author choose to name this story Grizzly Peak?*
    Look for literal reasons as well as more subtle, implied
    reasons, and cite supporting passages from the book.
    (CCSS.ELA-LITERACY.CCRA.R.4, CCSS.ELA-LITERACY.CCRA.R.5)

17. *Consider the story's setting. In what ways did the setting*
    drive the plot? Research other natural features you might find
    in the Canadian wilderness, and write a chapter incorporat-
    ing the new setting into Aaron and his dad's adventure.
    (CCSS.ELA-LITERACY.CCRA.R.3, CCSS.ELA-LITERACY.CCRA.R.6)

CPSIA information can be obtained
at www.ICGtesting.com
Printed in the USA
BVOW04*1447120317
478409BV00007B/157/P

J LONDON
London, Jonathan,
Grizzly Peak /
R2004443657 SDY_SP

MAY   2017

Atlanta-Fulton Public Library